Praise for *Trust me, I'm a Troublemaker*

'When Archie finally stands up to Miranda . . . the
confrontation makes for high powered fiction.'
Times Educational Supplement

'There are characters here that every child
will recognise and every adult should
try to understand.' *Observer*

'This is a very cleverly crafted, fast flowing
comedy and the more subtle lessons in
growing up and trying to change people
won't be lost either.' *Carousel*

'Full of comedy, this book has a light touch
that can be so difficult to achieve.'
Teaching and Learning

'Excruciatingly funny.' *The Times*

'A clever re-working of Pygmalion.' *Funday Times*

'This is a lovely, funny book which explores
the idea of misfits and labelling people in
a wonderfully entertaining way.'
School Librarian

Trust me, I'm a
Troublemaker

Pete Johnson

CORGI YEARLING BOOKS

TRUST ME, I'M A TROUBLEMAKER

A CORGI YEARLING BOOK 0 440 86770 3

Published in Great Britain by Corgi Yearling,
an imprint of Random House Children's Books

This edition published 2005

Copyright © Pete Johnson, 2005
Illustrations © Nigel Baines, 2005

The right of Pete Johnson to be identified as the author of this
work has been asserted in accordance with the Copyright, Designs
and Patents Act 1988.

Papers used by Random House Children's Books are natural,
recyclable products made from wood grown in sustainable forests.
The manufacturing processes conform to the environmental
regulations of the country of origin.

Set in 14/15½pt Century Schoolbook
by Falcon Oast Graphic Art Ltd.

Corgi Yearling Books are published by Random House Children's Books,
61–63 Uxbridge Road, London W5 5SA,
a division of The Random House Group Ltd,
in Australia by Random House Australia (Pty) Ltd,
20 Alfred Street, Milsons Point, Sydney, NSW 2061, Australia,
in New Zealand by Random House New Zealand Ltd,
18 Poland Road, Glenfield, Auckland 10, New Zealand
and in South Africa by Random House (Pty) Ltd,
Isle of Houghton, Corner of Boundary Road & Carse O'Gowrie,
Houghton 2198, South Africa

THE RANDOM HOUSE GROUP Limited Reg. No. 954009

www.kidsatrandomhouse.co.uk

A CIP catalogue record for this book is available from the British
Library.

Printed and bound in Great Britain by
Cox & Wyman Ltd, Reading, Berkshire.

To Gwynneth Bailey and all pupils at
Aldborough Primary School, with my
very best wishes.

MIRANDA JONES

Aunty Prue
Problem Solver Page
WOW
Williams Terrace
London

Tuesday January 6th

Dear Aunty Prue,
 I never thought I'd be writing to a
problem page. But you claim to answer
every letter – and you're my very last
hope.
 Tragedy entered my life last October.
 That's when I first clapped eyes on
Archie Swift. He stood in the playground
with an umbrella under one arm, a
newspaper under the other and some
tragic tat round his neck (a revolting
grey scarf with pom poms at the bottom
– if you want the gory details).
 He wasn't at all shy and before
registration we all knew his dad was

an actor whose greatest achievement was being the voice of Mr Wizzy in all those adverts ('No one wizzes through your loo faster than Mr Wizzy').

By the end of the first day we were already sick of Archie Swift - especially the way he had to stick his nose into absolutely everything. If he wasn't telling us what to do, he was tutting at us. I've never met a tuttier twelve year old. But then, he is way above the rest of us. In his eyes, anyway.

He's also the biggest crawler you've ever seen. He'll actually volunteer to wipe the blackboards for teachers and carry their trays back at lunchtime ... well, you get the idea, Aunty Prue.

Of course he never, ever, messes about in school. Once I flung him a water bomb and said, 'In the name of fun, Archie, throw that at someone. You can even throw it at me if you like.'

But he just gave me this puzzled look and asked, 'And what's the point of doing that?'

After that, I had no choice but to hurl the water bomb at him.

He is driving everyone insane, but

especially me. Just hearing his patronising voice warbling on and on is enough to bring up my breakfast.

But today (the first day back after Christmas) he plunged to new depths of awfulness. It was the last lesson and it looked as if Mrs Byrne had forgotten to set us any homework. We were all counting down to the bell when this slow, heavy, voice (he always speaks as if he's about eighty-seven years old) said, 'Excuse me, Mrs Byrne, but it's a homework night.'

The whole class tore into him afterwards – especially me. But he wasn't at all ashamed of himself. 'I had to do it,' he said, then gave this grizzly little smile. And I wanted to knock all his teeth out so badly.

He's a bod, of course. The most annoying bod on the face of this planet. And I can't take anymore. So what should I do?

Yours desperately,
Troublemaker
(also known as Miranda Jones)

Chapter One

From the pages of Archie's Diary

TUESDAY JANUARY 6TH

Got called a 'bod' again today. Also, a 'stupid creep', 'a suck-up', 'teacher's pet', and various other things I'd rather not repeat. And all because I reminded Mrs Byrne that it was a homework night.

'Why couldn't you keep your big trap shut?' screamed Miranda Jones at me afterwards.

But that just isn't my way, as I tried to explain.

It really isn't easy being exceptionally mature for your age. I haven't even hit thirteen yet and already I have the wisdom of an eighteen year old. Maybe even a twenty-one year old.

But then, I have always been highly advanced. At just six years old, I could converse with my nan and her friends about current affairs. They were so impressed. The funny thing is, I've never tried to act grown up. It's just that as soon as I wake up I can feel all this maturity bubbling up inside me.

It's a kind of gift, I suppose. Just like some people are born maths geniuses or football champions, I've been given a few extra helpings of wisdom.

Back at home it was my washing night. All the clothes are drying on the radiators as I write this. I shall get the ironing board out and attempt a few shirtsleeves before I go to school tomorrow.

Dad was late tonight. Another audition. But I had a proper cooked meal ready: chips, fish fingers and beans. There's always something hot waiting for him.

WEDNESDAY JANUARY 7TH
Gave Miranda a friendly greeting this morning. I wanted to show that I didn't bear a grudge about her screaming yesterday.

She immediately demanded, 'What are you doing?'

'Smiling at you.'

'Well, don't,' she replied. 'It disturbs me.'

That's her weird sense of humour, I expect. She's quite an odd person altogether, actually. She sits on her own at the back of the class, and looks a bit of a mess. She's always being told off for rolling up her skirt, or wearing trousers, or piercing her eyebrows (she got suspended for that last month).

We met our new maths teacher today: a smallish man with ginger hair and a little ginger moustache. He wrote his name on the blackboard. Mr Tinkler. Someone called out, 'Tinky Winky'. He went bright red, but he didn't say anything.

He spoke very quietly, but what he said was dead interesting. He said maths is a very exciting subject, but that some people get lost and that's why they don't enjoy it. 'Maths is like a journey,' he said. 'I shall lead you by the hand on this journey.'

'Oooh-er,' muttered someone.

'What about if you get travel sick?' said someone else.

Mr Tinkler went bright red again.

'Give him a chance,' I hissed. But they just sniggered. I can buy cheese that's more mature than some of my classmates.

THURSDAY JANUARY 8TH

Poor Mr Tinkler. One boy asked to be excused. And then six left. 'Not all at once,' he cried. But they went anyway. They were gone ages. It was the headmaster who brought them back. The class went completely silent when he slowly walked in.

The headmaster stood by the door watching the rest of the lesson. Mr Tinkler's hand shook when he started writing on the blackboard.

Afterwards I tried to have a friendly word with him. But the headmaster was hovering by his desk. He stayed talking to Mr Tinkler for most of the lunch hour. I really hope Mr Tinkler hasn't been given the sack or anything, as I feel he's got great potential.

FRIDAY JANUARY 9TH

4.30 p.m.

Mr Tinkler came into our classroom today like a different person. He burst in as if he'd just been let out of a trap. Then he made us all queue up outside the door and file in, in silence. 'Right, turn to your next clean page.' He sounded out of breath.

'Tinky Winky,' called out someone.

'Who said that?' he demanded. But no one owned up.

His moustache quivered. 'I want to make it absolutely clear. I won't tolerate this behaviour in my classroom. Not ever.'

He began writing on the blackboard. A boy at the back was secretly drinking from a can. Suddenly the can flew out of his hand and landed right by Miranda Jones's desk.

Mr Tinkler whirled round, spotting the can at once. 'Is that yours?' he asked her.

She shook her head.

'What's your name?'

She told him — and he pounced on it. He'd obviously heard it before, probably from another teacher.

'Stand up,' he demanded.

'Why?'

'Just do as you're told.'

She got to her feet very slowly. Then she stared at him, a faint amused smile on her lips.

'Right,' he barked, suddenly. 'I've had enough of this lack of respect. Just get out.' No one had been expecting that.

'I'll see you at the end of the lesson, Miranda Jones.'

'I'll count the moments,' she murmured

14

and then slouched towards the door.

'Anyone wish to join her?' he cried.

No one did. The whole class was now deathly quiet. Mr Tinkler banged his papers down on the desk. 'I will be treated with respect,' he cried. 'Rest assured of that.'

An air of tenseness hung over the rest of the lesson. I felt just a little sorry for Miranda Jones having to deal with Mr Tinkler when he was in such a ferocious mood.

To try and lighten things I gave him a friendly grin as I was leaving and asked, 'How are you settling in?'

He looked somewhat started. 'All right,' he muttered cautiously.

'Well, the first week is the worst. Once you've got that under your belt you'll be fine. Enjoy.' I believe my little chat relaxed him considerably.

But later Miranda Jones yelled across the playground at me. 'You just can't help yourself, can you? You've got to crawl to every single teacher in this school.' She'd completely misunderstood what I was trying to do.

This happens to me a lot, actually.

6.00pm

I'm back. Not to tell you anything else about school, it's Friday night, for goodness sake! But to give you a little tour of my bedroom. So don't be shy – come in.

First you'll notice all the aeroplanes dangling from the ceiling. Then you'll see a large football (my best sport), binoculars (I'm dead keen on bird-watching), and masses and masses of books, most of them passed down from Nan and her friends. I get through about three a week. Right now I'm reading a story about world domination and hypnotism called *The Three Hostages* by John Buchan.

On the walls are posters and some very personal photographs. So there's one of me as a baby being held by my mum. She passed away when I was seven months old, but in that picture she looks incredibly beautiful. I look like a giant boiled egg.

After she died Dad and I moved in with my mum's mother, Nan. She lives in Maidenhill, a smallish town, in Gloucestershire. She is quite bossy and her teeth click every time she eats, but I loved living with her. The only trouble was, Dad spent so much time travelling to auditions I hardly saw him some weeks.

Still, I spent many happy hours with Nan and her friends. Then last October, Dad told me that thanks to Mr Wizzy, we could afford to move closer to London. I looked forward to us having our own abode, but I hated being so far away from Nan.

She knitted me a scarf as a farewell gift which I wear every single day. There are two pictures of her on the wall, as well as one of me energetically tap-dancing. Nan introduced me to that particular pleasure.

In one corner of my room there's a little desk which wobbles like mad. And, of course, there's my very soft bed – and that's it really. Yet, when I've had a stressful day (like today) I come in here and let my bedroom cast its spell over me.

It never lets me down.

SATURDAY JANUARY 10TH
10.30 p.m.

Dad and I were innocently watching television tonight when up popped Mr Wizzy. 'It's new, it's brilliant,' he began. Suddenly Dad shot to his feet. He pointed a quivering hand at the television screen. He was too overcome with shock to speak.

Then horror seized me too, as I realized something terrible: Mr Wizzy now spoke with the voice of another actor.

'Can you believe it?' cried Dad. 'I've been dumped – and without anyone even bothering to let me know. Just wait until I speak to my voice agent!'

4.00 a.m.
Was woken about two hours ago by sounds from downstairs. I discovered Dad sitting in the kitchen, his hair sticking up, a haunted look on his face. 'Hey, I didn't mean to wake you.'

'Sometimes, Dad, there are more important things in life than sleeping,' I replied. I made us a late-night snack. It was one of my specialities: spaghetti with bacon bits. Then we had a long chat.

'To be honest, Archie,' said Dad, 'I was banking on that Mr Wizzy money for a few more months yet. Especially as nothing else is working out. I just go to lots of auditions, have nice things said to me, get incredibly hopeful and then watch someone else getting picked.'

'You've come a very close second a few times,' I said.

Dad brushed that aside. 'Sometimes I

wonder if I should forget the whole thing and get a proper job . . . it's just that I know there's a good actor inside me.'

'Say aah, and I'll find him for you,' I joked.

Dad smiled at that, then asked, 'Be honest now, Archie, am I wasting my time? I can take it.'

'Of course you're not,' I cried. 'You just need that lucky break, then your talent will burst out. And everyone will be so impressed, you'll never be out of work again. So keep going, Dad. I think success will happen for you quite soon now.'

'Got a feeling, have you?'

'That's right.' (I really have, by the way.)

Then Dad said, 'Some fathers are forever tearing their hair out over their sons. But I never have to worry about what your teachers are going to say about you . . . I'm so lucky.'

Actually, Dad and I are not a typical father and son at all. We're more like two really good mates.

SUNDAY JANUARY 11TH

Dad cheered up today. In fact, at the supermarket this afternoon he got into one of his wacky moods. He said I had just five minutes to fill my trolley with everything I wanted and my time started now.

So I raced around the aisles, while Dad started counting down in this extremely loud voice. Everyone was watching. One lady asked Dad what was going on. 'Speed shopping,' cried Dad. 'It's the latest thing. You'll be doing it soon.'

When we got back I made a sticky toffee pudding, which Dad dubbed a 'cosmic taste sensation'. He also said he'd take me wherever I wanted to go next Saturday. I chose the London Dungeon. I've been there before – and it never disappoints.

MONDAY JANUARY 12TH

Dad's voice agent said the advertisers felt Mr Wizzy needed 'freshening up'. This included a fresh voice.

While he was away this evening (at another audition) I threw out all the free Mr Wizzy products we'd been given. Now, nothing in our house will remind Dad of this chapter in his life.

TUESDAY JANUARY 13TH

In Mr Tinkler's lesson a girl was talking while he was writing on the blackboard. 'Be quiet, Miranda,' he said, without even turning round – and she was absent today! Someone tried to point this out, but he just snapped, 'Put your hand down. I'm not interested.' His face seems to be set in a mask of ill-temper now.

No one enjoys Mr Tinkler's lessons – not even me. But then, maths is my very worst subject.

Still, I always try to have a friendly word with him. Often I will mention something I have read in the paper that day. I think he appreciates my insights.

At lunchtime today I couldn't help noticing how messy the school was looking. Then I had a colossal brainwave. Why not ask each pupil to pick up just five pieces of litter? That way the whole school would be clear of rubbish in about thirty seconds.

I got very excited. So did Mrs Byrne, my form teacher, when I mentioned it to her. She said my scheme could transform our whole environment. I shall announce it tomorrow.

Chapter Two

WEDNESDAY JANUARY 14TH

5.00 p.m.

I explained my ambitious plan in assembly, then asked everyone to meet me at the back of the school at 12.30. All morning people were coming up to me and saying things like, 'I'm not picking up someone else's litter.' And, 'Why don't you just let the teachers do it?'

By half past twelve I had attracted an extremely large audience – and exactly one volunteer. He asked. 'Do we get an extra pudding for doing this?' When I informed him that we didn't, he hastily departed.

'Honestly,' I cried, 'I'm only asking you to pick up five pieces of litter.' People immediately started mimicking me, saying, 'I'm only asking you to pick up five pieces of litter.' I realized further dialogue was futile. So, I started filling up one of the large litter bins on my own. I was certain they'd all get bored of watching me doing this. But instead, even more people thronged about.

One boy dropped a crisp packet beside me. 'You forgot this,' he said. Someone else very helpfully tipped up all the rubbish I'd just been collecting. I didn't react though. I just carried on with my labours until this great tidal wave of pupils surged towards me, lifted me up into the air and then hurled me into the rubbish bin. Gave me quite a start.

I tried to maintain some dignity – not easy when you're addressing your audience sitting inside a bin – by saying, 'All right, you've had your joke.'

I was interrupted by Miranda Jones shouting at me, 'You're not a teacher.'

'I know,' I replied.

'Then why do you always try to act like one?'

'I'm merely trying to improve the quality of your life,' I replied. For some reason they all laughed uproariously at this comment.

Shortly afterwards a teacher appeared and I was able to scramble out of the bin and resume my work. But I was completely bewildered by what had happened. How could my superb idea have attracted such hostility?

Feel more than a bit depressed about it all, actually.

7.30 p.m.
Confession time: Sometimes I get fed up of being mature all on my own. I know one day some pupils will start to catch me up. I just wish they'd hurry up, then I could have stimulating conversations with them about . . . current affairs and the novels of John Buchan and Sir Arthur Conan Doyle, and the joys of bird-watching and . . . well so many other things, as I'm an excellent conversationalist. Also, I wish they'd stop calling me 'Bod'. It isn't funny and it isn't my name. But if I ask them to desist they'll just do it all the more, won't they? I feel as if I'm on the other side of the fence from them all the time.

THURSDAY JANUARY 15TH
Mr Tinkler gave an assembly this morning on photography – which is his big hobby,

apparently. He was surprisingly interesting and relaxed too. But in maths he just went back to being all tetchy and tense again.

This afternoon the headmaster asked to see me. He's a massive white-haired man and his office is about the size of a football pitch. He wanted to congratulate me for my efforts yesterday in sorting out the school's litter problem. As he was talking to me, he was also watering his plants. There were so many of them it was like he had his own private forest.

We talked away for ages. I think he felt quite relaxed in my company. Most adults do. Then he asked me about my hobbies. I very casually mentioned tap-dancing. He got very excited. He even put down his watering can.

He said the current theme of school assemblies was the hidden talents of teachers and pupils. So it would be wonderful if I could give a brief tap-dancing demonstration next Tuesday.

I quickly thought about this. Now, I believe my fellow pupils have got a rather serious image of me. They don't know about my fun side. Also, when I danced for Nan's friends they said I'd really brightened their day. And I like brightening people's days – so I've agreed. I've already started practising. I think next Tuesday could be a turning point for me at this school.

FRIDAY JANUARY 16TH

Miranda Jones was sent out of Tinkler's class again today. He said he didn't like her attitude. She replied that she wasn't wild about his attitude either.

She has certainly got a nerve!

Later she said, 'Once teachers slap a label on you, that's it. None of them ever see beyond it again.'

Trying to strike a more hopeful note I said, 'I don't think he's as bad as that. If you just had a quiet word with Mr Tinkler . . .'

'Bod' she snarled. 'Do you want a massive slap?'

'No, thank you.'

'Well, if you don't stem the tide of nonsense pouring out of your squiffy little mouth, you'll get one.'

You just can't help some people, can you?

SATURDAY JANUARY 17TH

Dad and I went to the London Dungeon in the morning. But the trip was spoilt by something he told me. He said, 'This'll make you laugh.' But it didn't. Instead, it worried me greatly.

Dad announced that this evening he is going to a club for unattached professionals. 'Just thought I'd go and meet some new faces,' he said.

But I wasn't fooled. He's hoping to find a lady he can go out on dates with, isn't he? I know about such matters.

But Dad is nearly thirty-four and should have grown out of all that business years ago.

Personally, I blame Mr Wizzy. Dad is still racked with despair about losing that role. So now he's going off the rails a bit.

And I'm not at all sure what to do.

SUNDAY JANUARY 18TH

3.30 p.m.

Guess what! Dad met a lady at that dating place. She's called Catherine and she knows one of our neighbours, who she just happens to be visiting this afternoon. And Dad's told her 'to swing round here afterwards'.

He asked me if I minded. What could I say? I'd never stop him having his friends round. Even though I think this whole venture is very ill-advised.

Back soon.

9.00 p.m.
At four o'clock I made some cheese dips and put out two bowls of nuts in the sitting room. Meanwhile, Dad got the fire going. He thought it might add atmosphere. It certainly added heat.

'It's going to be very informal,' he said, sweating there in his shirt, tie and smart trousers. When the doorbell rang he jumped a bit and asked, 'Hey, would you mind answering that, Archie? Give me a chance to compose myself. I'm a bit out of practice with all this.'

So I opened the door. 'Good night . . . I mean . . . good evening,' I said, getting flustered. She was younger than I'd expected. 'I am Archie,' I explained, 'the son of the man you have come here to visit.'

'Oh, hello there,' she said. She seemed nervous too. 'I'm Catherine.' And I liked the way she told me her first name right away.

Then I remembered something Nan had said to do to put visitors at their ease. 'Come on then, take your coat off so you feel the benefit later.'

She handed me her coat which I put over my arm, just as I'd seen butlers do in films. 'I hope you'll enjoy yourself tonight, Catherine,' I said. 'And when you wish for tea, coffee or hot chocolate, I'll be pleased to oblige you.'

Inside the sitting room the heat hit you at once. Dad came forward wearing one of his exaggerated smiles, which can be quite alarming when first encountered. 'Catherine, good to see you. Please excuse the mess . . . all-male household alert.'

'No, it's very nice,' she said. She looked around while Dad and I stood grinning away at her. She paused in front of the framed pictures on the wall (all put up by me, incidentally).

'I didn't know you were in *Grange Hill*,' she cried, excitedly. 'Who did you play?'

'The one who was always slightly out of focus,' replied Dad. 'I didn't say a lot, but I was part of the cast for three whole years.'

'And is this one of you in *Casualty*?'

'It is. I had leprosy or cataracts or something. . . but who cares anyway?' He laughed.

'Actually, he was very good,' I said.

'My biggest fan . . . in fact, my only fan.' Dad laughed wildly again.

When I left them Catherine was still looking rather tense, but I was certain once she'd sampled my cheese dips she'd unwind a bit.

But actually, she left shortly afterwards.

'She didn't stay very long,' I said. 'Afraid she'd melt away in the heat, was she?'

Dad smiled. 'I just went to pieces. I knew I was gibbering away talking total nonsense. That was like the worst audition I've ever done.'

Later, Dad and I laughed about it together like the two excellent mates we are. I think he realizes now that he's well past his time for going out with ladies. But it doesn't matter as I'll never abandon him. He'll always have me.

MONDAY JANUARY 19TH
Big rebellion at school today!

We were queuing up outside Mr Tinkler's room when Miranda Jones declared that we should all refuse to go inside until he started treating us like human beings. She said that it was time for us to make a stand.

So when Mr Tinkler opened the door and barked, 'Right, come in,' no one moved. Not even me. You could say I was temporarily hypnotised by Miranda Jones's magnetic personality.

He put his head round the door again. 'Which part of that last instruction didn't you understand? Come in!' He shouted those last two words and disappeared once more.

My deep maturity started rising to the surface. 'I'm sorry, but we can't stay out in the corridor any longer,' I said.

'Oh yes, we can,' snapped Miranda Jones. 'And we won't go in until he mends his ways.'

'You'll only make him even angrier than usual,' I replied. And I started walking regretfully, but purposefully, towards the classroom. Strong words followed me – the strongest from Miranda Jones. As I got to the door, a foot shot out and down I went.

Mr Tinkler watched me crashing into his classroom with some bewilderment.

'Good morning,' I said, scrambling to my feet.

'Where's everyone else?' he barked.

'Well, actually,' I said, trying to break the news as gently as I could, 'they won't

31

be joining us right now.'

Mr Tinkler goggled at me. 'What!'

'It's a protest, I'm afraid.' Then, trying to be the peacemaker, I added, 'Pardon my presumption but if you could be a tad more polite to everyone, and say please and thank you occasionally and . . .'

Mr Tinkler's face was now turning a very alarming shade of red. So, for the sake of his health (and mine) I stopped there.

After vigorously clearing his throat he strode to the door and bellowed, 'You've got two choices. You either begin your lesson right now or I shall march you all off to the headmaster's office immediately. Which is it to be?'

His voice was so loud even the chairs began rattling, and I wasn't very surprised when moments later people started trailing in. Finally, only one person remained outside: Miranda Jones. Then she too sailed in, her collar up, her nostrils flaring defiantly. Everyone else, though, looked distinctly crushed.

Mr Tinkler banged the class register down onto his desk. Just as I'd feared, Miranda Jones's protest had only served to put him in a grimmer mood. 'You've wasted ten minutes of my time, so I shall waste an hour of your time tomorrow. Class detention for everyone, except you, Archie.'

This did nothing to improve my popularity. In fact, my new nickname for the rest of the day was 'strike-breaker'. Made a change from 'Bod', I suppose. I also had pencils flicked at me and someone even stole my scarf. (To my great surprise, Miranda Jones was the person who told them to give it back)

Still, just wait until they get an eyeful of my tap-dancing tomorrow. I've been practising every night. If I say so myself, they've got a treat coming up.

TUESDAY JANUARY 20TH

I got up on the stage in assembly this morning in front of the whole of my year group. Above the loud beating of my heart I briefly explained that Nan was the one who'd introduced me to the wonderful world of dance and that I'd been tap-dancing since I was four years old. Everyone listened in stunned silence. This was a side to me that I don't think they'd ever guessed at.

'Now, let me entertain you,' I said. I put on my music (*Happy Feet*) and the performance began. I danced with considerable energy – well, at first I did. But soon I could hear people whispering and giggling. Then someone shouted, 'Get off'.

I was determined not to be put off and hoped my sheer artistry would win them over. Instead, a large sandwich whizzed over in my direction. It only very narrowly missed me. Other objects started flying in my direction until a teacher sprang up in front of me and led me away to safety. He gave everyone a big lecture about their appalling behaviour, while I just stood there in my tap shoes, dying of shame.

Afterwards came all the puerile questions, such as, 'Do you like going tap-dancing with your nan, then?' They all thought they were being so amusing. But I shan't ever dance for them again. So they're the losers really, aren't they?

A reply from Aunty Prue

Dear Troublemaker,

What to do about the bod in your class who annoys you so much? Absolutely nothing.

It's not his fault that he irritates you. You've got to try and bury your feelings and be kind to him.

No, it isn't easy, but in the long term it is worth the effort. You never know, one day you might even discover that he is quite an interesting person after all.

Come on, give him a chance.

Best wishes,

Aunty Prue

MIRANDA JONES

Aunty Prue
Problem Solver Page
WOW
Williams Terrace
London

Tuesday January 20th

Hey, Aunty Prue,
So, you're not a fake. You really do
answer your letters. And what a flashy
autograph!
   But, at the risk of sounding ungrate-
ful, the advice you gave me was totally
lousy. All that waffle about Archie
being quite interesting really. He's
about as interesting as a boiled sweet.
   And since I last wrote he's become
even worse.
   For instance, we've got this new

teacher at our school called Tinkler:
ginger mullet, pointy yellow teeth,
cheese and onion breath and the
manners of a baboon. Just awful. Worst
of all, he picks on people for no reason,
especially me.

So I organized a protest. We all
refused to step inside his hellhole until
he'd mended his ways. And it was going
brilliantly until you-know-who just had
to break the strike. If he goes five
minutes without creeping to a teacher
his stomach will explode. The whole
protest was ruined because of him!

To top it all, today he starts prancing
about in assembly to some scratchy old
song. And you can tell he thinks he's
marvellous. Of course, the teachers were
gazing at him with expressions of
ecstasy on their ancient faces. But for
everyone else it was just totally
painful.

In the end a few objects were thrown
as a small protest. After which a
teacher creaked to his feet and said
Archie didn't deserve such treatment.
And, to be fair, he didn't. He deserved
to be kicked very hard for what he'd
inflicted on us.

People are now doing things like stealing his scarf. I think that's a bit petty. There's got to be a better way to make Archie see the error of his ways.

But what is it?

Come on, Aunty Prue, Send some ideas.

Yours ever more desperately,

Miranda (alias Troublemaker)

← desperate

Chapter Three

WEDNESDAY JANUARY 21ST

You won't believe this, but Dad's off on another date on Friday. A woman he met briefly at that singles place found out his phone number from someone else and rang him up. She's called Cheryl and she sounds extremely forward to me. But Dad's chuffed to bits about it all and is meeting her for a drink.

I do worry about him.

THURSDAY JANUARY 22ND

Told Nan about Dad's date on Friday. She was very interested.

She said, 'Your father's at a difficult age, Archie.'

'Oh, is he? I didn't know that,' I replied.

'So how long does this difficult age last?'

I think Nan said, 'The rest of his life', but I can't be sure, as she just murmured that. She went on, 'We'll just have to be patient with him, won't we?'

FRIDAY JANUARY 23RD

Dad's back from his date with Cheryl. He didn't say much which probably meant it was another disaster. But I didn't probe. I believe in allowing parents their privacy.

SUNDAY JANUARY 25TH

Dad saw that Cheryl again tonight. He'd bought tickets for the cinema but in the end they didn't go. They were too busy gassing in the wine bar. Talk about wasting your money.

MONDAY JANUARY 26TH

Today Dad's auditioning for a new soap on satellite TV called *Rivals*. I said to him I've got a feeling this could be it – his breakthrough.

WEDNESDAY JANUARY 28TH

Dad thinks he'd have heard by now if he'd got the part. We're both extremely disappointed.

THURSDAY JANUARY 29TH

Just reached an important decision and wanted you to be the first to know. I've been thinking about school and I now realize I'm not cut out for it. Just as some pupils have trouble fitting in because they're extremely gifted ... I have a similar problem because of my vast maturity.

There's only one solution. I must leave school and be taught at home instead. Of course I realize money is rather tight now. But it needn't be someone expensive – any wise person will do. And one day, when the pupils' maturity count increases I shall, of course, return.

I've got to wait for the right moment before telling Dad of my plan. But I'm sure he'll agree.

THURSDAY FEBRUARY 5TH

6.00 p.m.
Yes, I know, it's been a while. In fact, a whole week has ambled by since I last wrote. But I wanted to wait until I had something really good to tell you. And now, at long last, I have.

DAD HAS GOT A PART IN *Rivals*. It wasn't the one he auditioned for – it's a completely different one. But who cares? Dad's on his way to stardom at last. Isn't that BRILLIANT NEWS?

Dad opened a bottle of wine, and let me have a small glass. We drank a toast to Mum.

'I wish she knew about this,' said Dad.

'Maybe she does,' I replied.

A tear leaked out of Dad's eyes when I said that. But I pretended not to notice. Now we're going to have a celebration meal.

7.00 p.m.
Over the meal Dad told me Cheryl might pop round tonight. 'She was just so pleased when I told her about *Rivals*.'

I can't think why. Dad's only known her for five minutes, for goodness sake.

9.45 p.m.
At eight o'clock I was just putting out the milk bottles when this figure came bursting out of the mist. It was Cheryl.

'You must be Archie,' she said, stretching out a hand.

Then she bounded into the house and gave Dad a long, slurpy kiss. I suppose she wasn't bad-looking. She had quite nice

42

hair (long and blonde) and a smiley expression which seemed to be stuck on her face. I just wish she didn't stink of perfume.

She went whirring round the house peering in all the rooms (yes, including mine) which I thought was rather rude of her.

Despite my misgivings, I tried to be a good host and engage her in polite conversation. She was quite frank. She told me she was separated from her husband so she and her daughter, Eliza, were moving out of their house to a much smaller one. I nearly felt sorry for her.

But then she charged into the kitchen and started examining our rota. Here I list all the household chores which Dad and I need to perform every day.

'So whose turn is it to clean out the loo tomorrow?' she asked, winking at Dad.

Afterwards, Dad said, 'Isn't she great?'

'I guess so,' I replied, but very quietly.

10.15 p.m.
I've just remembered it's a no-school-uniform day at school tomorrow. Clothes are totally unimportant to me. My mind is on much more important things. But I

know if I wear my old blue jumper and brown trousers there'll be snide comments ... so I shall turn up in my usual school clothes. I bet I'll be the only one in uniform tomorrow.

Aunty Prue
Problem Solver Page
WOW
Williams Terrace
London

THURSDAY FEBRUARY 5TH

Hey Aunty Prue,
   Don't bother trying to think up a
solution to my problem, (namely, Archie)
as I've just come up with one.
   We were all talking about this no
school-uniform day and someone
wondered what Archie was going to
wear. And that's when my brain cells
blazed into action.
   Here's the plan: two boys and I will
come to school as Archie. Not only will
we wear clothes in his style, but we'll

copy all his many, many irritating
habits for one whole day. That way,
Archie will see for himself how useless
and ghastly he is - and start changing
immediately.

You've got to admit, Aunty Prue, my
plan's better than what you suggested.
But please don't be too depressed. At
least you had a go.

There's no need to reply now as I'm
all sorted - though I'd really like it if
you did.

Luck and stuff,

Miranda

Miranda (alias Troublemaker)

♡ ☆ ☆ ◎

Chapter Four

FRIDAY FEBRUARY 6TH

This has been, without doubt, the weirdest day of my whole life.

I thought I'd be the only person at school in uniform today. Well, I wasn't. Just as I arrived I saw Andy Bailey and Craig Stevens in full school uniform. They were also wearing long scarves and both had newspapers under their arms. Distinctly intrigued now, I followed them to Mrs Byrne's classroom. I heard Andy Bailey call out, 'Good morning, miss, got any little jobs you want doing before school starts?' His voice sounded different: he was talking very slowly for some reason.

Then a third person strode over towards them – Miranda Jones. To my total amazement she was also in uniform and wearing a scarf. She waved an umbrella at them. 'You've both forgotten the brolly.'

At once my face burned red with shock and embarrassment. I knew what they were doing – they were dressing up as me.

Then I was spotted and Andy Bailey called out, 'All hail to our leader.'

I didn't know how to reply to that so I just asked, 'What exactly are you doing?'

'We're going to be bods for a day,' cried Miranda.

In the classroom no one was surprised to see these three dressed up as me – except Mrs Byrne. 'Why are you in uniform?' she demanded.

'Because they're our favourite clothes in all the world,' replied Miranda in this slow, heavy voice (which, by the way, is nothing like mine). She went on, 'Mrs Byrne, may I ask you a question?'

'Yes,' she replied.

'Have you always been this fantastic or did you used to be not quite so fantastic?'

'I know when I'm having my leg pulled,' replied Mrs Byrne.

Andy Bailey jumped to his feet. 'Can I dance for everyone? Oh, please say I can.' He started thumping about, saying, 'I go up the social club with my nan every Friday. She's so hot—'

'All right, Andy,' interrupted Mrs Byrne. 'That's enough.'

The class were all laughing like mad hyenas now, but Mrs Byrne was staring rather anxiously at me. So I grinned back, showing I knew how to take a joke.

Mrs Byrne went on, 'I only wish you three came to school so neatly dressed every day. Have you ever done your top button up in your life before, Miranda?'

'But I do it up every morning, miss,' cried Miranda Jones. 'I take such pride in my appearance. I'd also just like to thank you for a very wonderful registration. The way you read those names out, so clear and bell-like – please accept this token of my esteem.'

And she rushed up and whacked a very large apple down on the desk.

'Go on, get out,' laughed Mrs Byrne.

Mr Tinkler was nowhere near as amused. Especially when Miranda raised her hand and asked, 'May I wash the windows for you or clean the board or lick your shoes?'

'Any more rudeness and you'll spend the rest of this lesson outside,' he said.

'But sir, I'd never be rude to you. I was only asking if I could help. That's what I live for: helping teachers.'

When the bell went for the end of the lesson Miranda let out a huge groan. 'Oh no, it can't be the end already. Can't we stay longer? We'd rather listen to you, Mr Tinkler, than go to boring old break, wouldn't we?' Her accomplices roared their agreement.

'I do not find your antics the slightest bit amusing,' said Mr Tinkler. But everyone else did. They fell about when the three of them copied my walk (I tend to keep my hands behind my back), and the little cough I do just before I'm going to speak. They even imitated the way I put all my pens out on the desk before every lesson.

At lunchtime I normally eat my sandwiches alone – but today the three impersonators jammed round the table with me.

'Does your nan do your packed lunch for you?' asked Craig Stevens.

'And does she put in a special sweet if you've been a good boy?' asked Andy Bailey. Without waiting for me to reply he pointed to his top button and made loud strangling noises. 'I don't know how you wear it like this every day.'

'How long will you continue with this?' I asked.

'You've only got to suffer us doing this for one day,' said Miranda. 'We have to put up with you every day.'

I laughed rather nervously. Even when Miranda's making a joke – as she surely was then – she can look rather grim.

At the end of the day Mrs Byrne asked me, 'You haven't minded their little bit of play-acting?'

'Oh no,' I said, hastily.

'Good lad,' she said. Then she added, 'Imitation is the sincerest form of flattery, you know.'

I suppose it was an odd kind of compliment. But why did they decide to do an impression of me? Apart from my immense maturity, I'm nothing special. So what was the point?

It must be one of their silly games . . .

SATURDAY FEBRUARY 7TH

Cheryl's just been here again. I attempted to discuss the fascinating subject of climate change with her. She looked a bit funny while I was talking. And afterwards she murmured. 'You've got a lot to say for yourself, haven't you?' Actually, I was just trying to fuel an interesting discussion. I fear my efforts fell on deaf ears.

Been thinking some more about those impressions of me. I've decided they were merely a laugh and a prank. Well, I've shown I can take a joke, haven't I?

SUNDAY FEBRUARY 8TH
Cheryl turned up again today. But this time I remained in my bedroom. I don't think she missed me. And I didn't miss her either.

The chilly fingers of school beckon but, for once, I'm almost looking forward to it.

In a way, you could say those impressions on Friday were a kind of tribute. And it shows my classmates do respect me – perhaps even like me a little.

MONDAY FEBRUARY 9TH
What a day!

I'd like to tell you more but I'm absolutely shattered.

TUESDAY FEBRUARY 10TH
Another great day. The trouble is, I'm falling asleep as I write this. Sorry.

WEDNESDAY FEBRUARY 11TH

Today was even better than yesterday. My hands are still trembling with the excitement of it all.

THE MOST ANNOYING BOD ON THE FACE OF THIS PLANET

Dear Aunty Prue,

Tragedy entered my life last October. That's when this boy darkened my school for the first time. He had an umbrella under one arm, a newspaper under the other and a revolting grey, scarf with pom poms, round his neck. By the end of the first day we were all sick of him and especially the way he had to stick his nose into everything. If he wasn't telling us what to do, he was tutting at us.

He's also the biggest crawler you've ever met. He even tells teachers when they forget to set homework.

He is, without doubt, the most annoying bod on the face of this planet. And I cannot take anymore. So what should I do? Unless you reply dead fast, I shall have assassinated him.

Signed,
Troublemaker

Aunty Prue says:

What to do about the bod in your class who annoys you so much? Absolutely nothing.

It's not his fault that he irritates you. You've got to try and bury your feelings and be kind to him.

No, it isn't easy, but in the long term it is worth the effort. You never know, one day you might even discover he is quite an interesting person after all.

Come on, give him a chance.

Aunty Prue
Problem Solver Page
WOW
Williams Terrace
London

Wednesday February 11th

Hey Aunty Prue

Yes, it's me again - your favourite pen-pal. Ha Ha. I'm back because something awful has happened - and it's mainly your fault.

First of all, you remember my plan to make Archie less ghastly. Well, unfortunately the peabrain saw us pretending to be him as some kind of tribute! He went springing about on Monday morning thinking he was everyone's favourite. But a sensational shock lay in wait for him - courtesy of you.

I never thought you'd actually publish a bit of my letter, Aunty Prue. Especially as all the letters you usually print are about nail varnish or kissing boys or something equally trivial. It was a girl in my class who found it. She quickly sussed it was about Archie and that I was the author.

Soon it was the talk of the school. People laughed themselves senseless about it. And they were determined that Archie should see it. 'He's got to realize how annoying he is,' they said.

'Yes,' I said, 'but I don't think he should have to face a great mob of people. That's too raw - even for him.'

They agreed with me and then did it anyway. They surrounded him in the corridor, and then one girl thrust the problem page at him. 'Read this,' she ordered. And sixty pairs of eyes watched him as he did exactly that.

At the end, he asked, in a stunned voice, 'So I am the problem of the week?'

I wanted to reply, 'No, you're the problem of the year, mate.' But I didn't need to say anything. He looked right at me. Somehow he just knew I was the author of that letter. Then, without uttering another word, he staggered off.

At that moment, if someone had

handed me poison I'd have gulped it down and asked for seconds.

I felt truly dreadful.

Archie has stopped bouncing round the school – which is good. But instead, he drags himself from lesson to lesson in a shell-shocked manner, not speaking to anyone (no, not even the teachers). I tell you, he's even more irritating now than he was before.

Meanwhile, I am living in the land of the very guilty and I hate it there. Not that it's really my fault. If you'd warned me you were going to publish my letter... well, at least I'd have been prepared. Why didn't you?

And what should I do now? Tell me dead fast.

Thanks a million,

Miranda

Miranda (alias Troublemaker)

P.S. Don't bother posting me the free make-up kit as I think all make-up is pointless. You can keep it.

Chapter Five

THURSDAY FEBRUARY 12TH

6.00 p.m.

Will you do me a favour, please? Ignore the entries from Monday 8th to Wednesday 11th February, inclusive – as they contain nothing but dirty lies.

Lying to your own diary – how low is that? Let's just say, despair took over me on Monday and it still has me in its iron grip.

You see, I found out something terrible on Monday. There's this girls' magazine called *WOW* and it's got a problem page. This week's problem was about someone dubbed 'The most annoying bod on the face of the planet', and that's me.

You're shocked, aren't you? Well,

imagine how I felt. Miranda Jones wrote it on behalf of everyone at my school. When she and those boys dressed up as me it wasn't a merry tease – no, they were holding up a mirror of my many (in their opinion) irritating ways.

I knew they had difficulties with my adult bearing on life. But actually, it's much worse than that. Sad to relate, I am, in fact, deeply disliked by one and all.

Such news really saps your confidence – not to mention your sparkle. I also realize I'm just not right for school. I had, of course, thought this before, but now I know it's time. The sooner I leave, the better it will be for everyone.

6.15 p.m.
Still, I'm glad I've told you the truth. Now, once again, there are no secrets between us. And it's half term next week, which has got to be good news.

FRIDAY FEBRUARY 13TH
An unlucky day all right. Dad said to me tonight, 'Cheryl's in a bit of a mess.' He told me how she had to leave her house tomorrow, but couldn't move into her new one yet. He went on and on about how

badly she'd been let down. But actually, I couldn't have cared if she had to live in a hole in the road and eat coal for breakfast. (Sorry if that appals you, but I'm not keeping anything back now.)

In the end, I said, 'Well, she'll just have to book into a hotel.'

'That's a bit pricey, though,' said Dad. 'No, I was wondering if Cheryl and Eliza could stay with us . . . just until she gets settled.'

He must have noticed how my mouth had sprung open with shock, as he added, quietly, 'It'll only be for a few days . . . a week or two at the most. They'll just move into our spare room.'

'You know, Dad,' I said, 'I really think it might be better if you lent her the cash for a hotel. I mean, it's not a very big house—'

'But it'll be fun,' interrupted Dad. 'And I know Cheryl will help out. She's not someone to just sit back. Well, you've met her.'

'Yes, I've met her,' I said, slowly. I really wasn't happy about someone who we hardly knew being imported into our home. I decided to call in reinforcements. I rang Nan.

She was dead shocked. 'Typical man. He

just hasn't thought this through at all.'

'She might be a mad axe-murderer or a poisoner, mightn't she? We hardly know her,' I whispered.

'Don't worry,' said Nan. 'I'll speak to him.'

I was a bit more cheerful after that. Dad hardly ever disagrees with Nan – not to her face, anyhow.

He was in the bedroom when Nan called. But I could hear most of what he said, as he was talking quite loudly. Also, I had my ear right up against the door at the time.

Dad said, 'Of course I was going to tell you about it . . . it's just Archie got to you first. And it won't be for long . . . and she's really nice.'

I'm not sure what Nan said next but Dad's voice suddenly rose. 'Cheryl and I just clicked the moment we met. And she's been so supportive—'

Nan can't have been too impressed with this gush as Dad practically shouted, 'I'm very sorry you feel like that but you'll have to trust me on this one.'

I jumped away from the door, just as he pushed it open. I thought he might be cross with me for ringing Nan, but instead he patted me on the shoulder and said, 'I think some female company might do us good, shake us up a bit.'

But I've been shaken up enough this week.

They move in tomorrow.

SATURDAY FEBRUARY 14TH
5.00 p.m.

They arrived an hour ago. Dad and I had spent most of the day hoovering and cleaning 'their room' and generally getting ready to receive them.

Considering most of their stuff was being stored, they had enough suitcases. I took Cheryl's bags up for her then asked, 'Now, would you like a paper and an early morning call tomorrow?'

But Cheryl didn't smile. She hasn't tuned into my sense of humour yet.

Then I said, 'I was sorry to hear about your difficulties. When exactly will your new house be ready?'

Before she could reply Dad cut in, 'Hey, Archie, stop interrogating our guests.' He laughed in a very exaggerated way. Whenever women visit Dad goes over the top. I shall behave in a much more controlled way towards the opposite sex when I am his age.

Earlier today he'd received a Valentine card. It was a home-made one with ribbons and hearts glued onto it. Not signed, of course. But Cheryl blushed when he mentioned it, so we knew who the culprit was. Dad was highly evasive when I asked if he'd sent Cheryl one.

Eliza hasn't spoken a word yet. She just stood very close to Cheryl, clutching one of the bags, her eyes wide and staring. She looked as if she'd just arrived at the House of Terror.

Off to cook tea for everyone now.

8.00 p.m.
Made a right mess of the home-made cheese and onion pie, didn't I? Usually, it's one of my specialities. But today I didn't cook it properly, and as a consequence, it was all cold in the middle. I still felt Cheryl and Eliza could have attempted the non-cold part, which was extremely tasty.

It was hard concentrating on my cooking with Cheryl popping in and out of the kitchen every five seconds. I need privacy at such moments.

Eliza still hasn't spoken a word. Cheryl is now preparing a salad for Eliza and herself. I really don't care.

9.45 p.m.
I'd just sprawled out on the couch in the sitting room and was enjoying a few minutes peace when Cheryl looked in.

'Are you allowed to put your feet up on the furniture, Archie?' she asked.

What did she mean 'allowed'? Dad and I are a team, for goodness' sake. But I nodded my head.

'That is fine, then. But just thought I'd better check,' she said.

Why? What was it to do with her, anyway?

Shortly afterwards I went out for a walk in the cool night air. This calmed me down. Today has lasted for about twenty years.

SUNDAY FEBRUARY 15TH

Was woken up by Eliza skipping right outside my bedroom door. 'Hello,' I said to her. She didn't reply, just scurried away.

Came downstairs to discover Dad and Cheryl in the kitchen with their arms wrapped round each other. First thing in the morning you don't want to see aged people slobbering over each other. I coughed indignantly before enquiring, 'What would you like for breakfast, then?'

They immediately whirled round. And

Cheryl announced, 'No, I'm in charge this morning. I'm cooking us all some nice, healthy kippers. You go and watch cartoons.'

Cartoons! How old did she think I was?

Eliza was already in the sitting room. She'd settled herself on my favourite part of the sofa. She'd also taken control of the remote and kept flicking through all the channels. Halfway through breakfast she spoke to me for the very first time. 'You eat weird,' she announced.

'Thank you so much,' I replied.

I cooked the evening meal of sausages, chips and beans. Eliza took one look at it and said, 'Yuk, what's that?' Apparently she doesn't eat sausages or beans. And she isn't wild about chips either. So, of course, Cheryl had to make something else for her.

Later I heard Cheryl murmur to Dad that she was worried about the lack of vegetables in our diet.

I burst into the kitchen and cried, 'Aren't baked beans a vegetable? We have those practically every day.'

Cheryl just smirked at me.

MONDAY FEBRUARY 16TH
DISADVANTAGES OF HAVING CHERYL
AND ELIZA TO STAY

1) Fridge is now crammed with Cheryl and Eliza's food.
2) Bathroom is also full of their things. And I couldn't get into it for ages this morning.
3) Cheryl gives me funny looks when I read the newspaper at breakfast. She gives me funny looks at other times too. I'm really not sure why.
4) Eliza has been using my jar of Marmite. I know this, because I discovered bread-crumbs in it.
5) Eliza thinks the remote control belongs to her alone.
6) Eliza says she can't bear the way I chew my cereals or eat a packet of crisps. She could give me a complex for life. Just for the record: I close my mouth when I eat and have never in my entire life received any complaints before. When I mentioned this to Dad he just chortled and said, 'Oh, that's girls for you.'
7) Cheryl's perfume is giving me a nasty cough. I suspect I'm violently allergic to it.

ADVANTAGES OF HAVING CHERYL AND ELIZA TO STAY

Still thinking about that one.

TUESDAY FEBRUARY 17TH
MORE DISADVANTAGES

Eliza had two friends round today. They all kept following me about whispering and giggling. I felt like a guest in my own house. She also told them I had stinky feet – another slur which I strongly deny.

SOME ADVANTAGES

Forget it.

This evening Eliza rushed into my bedroom and switched all the lights off. Childish isn't the word! She did this twice more. Finally, just to teach her a lesson, I dashed into her room and switched the lights off. I really had no idea Cheryl was in there at the time. A few seconds later Cheryl put her head round my door and questioned me about the incident.

I owned up at once – but felt extremely embarrassed. As you know, I never usually indulge in such juvenile antics – but feel I was driven to it tonight.

THURSDAY FEBRUARY 19TH

When Dad's around Cheryl acts like the nicest person in the world. But when he's away rehearsing *Rivals* – like today – she gives off all the warmth of an ice cube.

All morning her eyes kept resting on me in an impatient sort of way, as if to say, 'Why are you still in this house?' Finally, she asked me, 'Don't you ever go and hang out with your mates?'

Highly personal stuff like that is really nothing to do with her, is it? But I replied, 'Well, actually, I don't socialize with people of my age very much. I've moved on from youth clubs and such things. I'm somewhat advanced for my years, I'm afraid.'

She just gave me a very thin smile in reply. Then she commenced hoovering the sitting room. I very politely pointed out that hoovering was on the rota as one of my tasks. She gave me an evil stare and said, very snappily, 'But I thought you'd be glad of some help. The house is really quite messy, you know.'

'Oh, I know that,' I shot back. 'In fact, it's so dirty that Dad and I spend most nights shooting all the rats who congregate here with an air gun.'

Those sarcastic words just flew out,

taking even me by surprise. I was absolutely furious. How dare she call our house messy? Nan was most impressed by my level of cleanliness when she visited at Christmas.

This evening Cheryl insisted we all have herbal tea, saying we'd discover how much more delicious it was than ordinary tea. In fact, it tasted of nettles and underpants. And I could only manage a mouthful before feeling violently ill. Cheryl gave me another evil stare when I announced this.

She is— NO, STOP. This diary is turning into a massive moan against Cheryl. And she'll be gone soon. Also, these days are the worst because I'm on half term, so is Eliza, and Cheryl has taken some days off work. Next week will be easier, when we are not cooped up here all the time, and then they'll be on their way.

So I'm banning any more moaning about Cheryl on these pages. I'm mature enough to stand her.

FRIDAY FEBRUARY 20TH

No, I'm not. And I'm breaking my ban right now – because Cheryl's just accused me of stealing.

A few minutes ago she came into my bedroom with a dead serious expression on her face. 'I bought four chocolate éclairs as a treat for us all tonight.'

I nodded. I'd seen them in the fridge.

'But now,' and here her voice rose accusingly, 'they're all gone.'

Well, not a crumb of them had passed my lips. So I just muttered, 'That's a shame.'

'Yes, it is,' she agreed. 'You can't help solve this little mystery, then?'

I shook my head.

'All right, thank you,' she said, extremely sniffily.

Five minutes later Dad came plodding up the stairs. He smiled apologetically at me and said, 'You and I are used to just helping ourselves out of the fridge whenever we feel like it, aren't we? But now we've got guests . . .'

I gaped at him in utter horror. It was bad enough Cheryl accusing me of thieving . . . but for my own father to join in. I burst out, 'I didn't even breathe on her mildewed, miserable chocolate eclairs.'

Dad stepped back from me in some alarm. He could see I was deeply anguished. 'Now look, it's obviously just a misunderstanding. I'll explain it all and no harm done, eh?'

'Yes, there is. My name has been stained by a false charge. And I must clear it NOW.'

7.25 p.m.
Eliza has just locked herself in the loo — and it's my fault, apparently.

All I did was cross-examine her about the chocolate eclairs. I was certain she'd eaten them, then blatantly tried to put the blame on to me. But instead of admitting her guilt and clearing up the whole ugly affair, she let out an almighty squawk and shot into the loo.

Cheryl went into a right flap, going on and on about Eliza having a very sensitive nature.

As I write this Cheryl is still calling things through the loo door, Dad looks totally shattered and I have retired to my bedroom.

7.45 p.m.
Eliza's out of the loo, if you were at all concerned, which I certainly wasn't. She's being treated as if she's just returned from a year in Siberia. And now Cheryl's saying,

'Look, they are only éclairs.' Her hypocrisy is mind-blowing!

Cheryl and Dad are downstairs humouring Eliza. I have declined to join them. I shall just remain in my bedroom for the rest of the evening.

Yet another very long day.

SATURDAY FEBRUARY 21ST
8.00 p.m.

There are some new cakes in the fridge and Cheryl has stuck a little note on to them. It says, 'Do not eat. A family treat. Thank you. C.'

I just know that's been penned for my benefit. And what does she mean 'family treat?' She's not part of my family. And never will be.

SUNDAY FEBRUARY 22ND

Cheryl and Eliza went out this afternoon so Dad and I had the house to ourselves. Brilliant.

I was able to discuss with Dad the matter of my academic future. I said, 'I think I have now reached a crossroads in my life regarding school . . . and it's time for a change of direction.'

Dad was looking totally bewildered. So I

asked, more simply, 'Could I leave school next week and have a tutor at home instead?'

'Aren't you happy at school?' asked Dad, looking most concerned.

'Oh yes,' I said, hastily. 'It's just that I'd be even happier away from it. And I think a tutor is the ideal solution. It needn't be a top of the range one. Anyone with a few qualifications and a pleasing personality would do.'

Dad looked right at me. 'Archie, you know you can tell me anything, don't you?'

I nodded.

'Are you having any problems at school?'

'Not at all.'

Dad went on looking at me.

'Well, only . . . that I irritate one or two people.'

'Who, exactly?'

If I listed them all we'd be here for the rest of the night. So I just said, 'I believe some pupils find me somewhat challenging,' my voice fell away, 'and annoying.'

'Annoying!' Dad whispered the word too. 'I don't see that.'

'Neither do I,' I smiled. 'But that's what they think. Not that I let it bother me. But

I would like a change from the daily grind of school. Of course, I could go back there in my later years – all refreshed. So, will you book me a tutor? You can take some of the costs out of my pocket money.'

Dad got up and ruffled my hair. 'Let me think about it, will you?'

I'm pretty hopeful, actually.

9.30 p.m.
By this time next week Cheryl and Eliza will have gone. Just writing that sentence puts a smile on my face. So do you mind if I write it out again? BY THIS TIME NEXT WEEK CHERYL AND ELIZA WILL HAVE GONE.

MONDAY FEBRUARY 23RD

In my bedroom I discovered a note from Cheryl. It said, 'I could not clean your room properly because of all the mess on the floor. C.'

I penned Cheryl a message back. 'Kindly refrain from cleaning my bedroom. That is my task on Wednesday nights, as you will see if you consult the rota on the kitchen wall. For your information, I keep stuff on my floor at all times. Thanking you for your interest. A.'

TUESDAY FEBRUARY 24TH

A very odd thing happened at school today. When Miranda Jones saw me a smile floated across her face. I was too shocked to know how to respond.

What on earth's going on?

A reply from Aunty Prue

Dear Miranda,

I'm sorry you were surprised to see your letter in WOW. Decisions about which letters to include are made quite late (and not only by me), so I wasn't able to let you know in advance.

But I doubt it's just the letter which has upset Archie so much. I was unhappy about your plan of dressing up as him. Making fun of people is never a good idea. Still, it is to your credit you recognize you have done something wrong.

What you must do now is very simple: talk to Archie and tell him you're sorry for any distress you've caused him. Also, maybe you could ask him if he needs any help. This won't be easy but perhaps it has to be done!

I am certain you can put things right.

Best wishes,

Aunty Prue

P.S. Thank you for the kind offer of the make-up kit, but it has already been sent to you. I am sure you will find someone else who would like it.

Aunty Prue
Problem Solver Page
wow
Williams Terrace
London

Tuesday February 24th

Dear Aunty Prue,
   Good of you to answer so fast. Shame
about the advice though.
   All that guff about talking to Archie
- I'm surprised you didn't ask me to
adopt him. No offence. And I'm sure
your advice would be great for kids who
adults call 'nice', like my sister, for
instance.
   But no one's ever called me 'nice'
and never will either. You see, I run
on anger and bolshiness. I'm always
challenging adults and arguing with

them. So they call me a 'troublemaker'.
If they don't like me - so what. I can't
do anything about that. Just as I can't
change the fact that my nose is too big.

But please don't think I'm unreason-
able. If I'm asked politely to do
something, I might just do it. But if
I'm told to do it, my hackles go up
right away. And once I'm picked on...

No one messes with me and gets away
with it as Tinkler is about to find out.
I feel I'm rambling now, but actually,
Aunty Prue, I did want to tell you
something. After reading your letter
this morning I went straight off and
smiled at Archie. Felt totally shattered
afterwards. I haven't been this kind to
anyone for years.

But I'm afraid that's as far as I can
go. I still feel bad about Archie, but I
don't do hugging, or apologising, or
talking things over. In fact, I'd sooner
stick my head in a pan of boiling chip
fat, than go through any of that. So-t

Chapter Six

WEDNESDAY FEBRUARY 25TH

I was putting my key in the lock tonight when I heard a crashing sound. I came through the door and saw that the little shelf in the hallway on which I'd arranged a selection of models was swinging on its side. Its contents were scattered right across the carpet.

My favourite ornament, a unicorn, was smashed to bits. Beside it was my football.

I knew at once who had removed the football from my bedroom without permission and had been hurling it about so destructively. I picked it up – a grave mistake, as you will shortly discover – and called out, 'Eliza'.

An innocent (!) face popped out from the

kitchen. 'Yes', she began. Then she gasped, 'Oh no, what have you been doing?'

Before I could reply Cheryl came rushing through the door. She immediately noticed the carnage on the carpet.

'Who did this?' she demanded.

'He did,' cried Eliza. 'I saw him. He was going mad down here with that football.'

'What rubbish,' I shouted back. 'You stole this ball from my private quarters and then—'

'No, I didn't!' she screamed.

'Yes, you did!' I yelled.

'Just stop!' screamed Cheryl. 'If I didn't have a headache before I came in here, I certainly have one now. You can both go upstairs this minute. I really can't listen to any more of this fighting.'

Eliza was already slipping upstairs. But I just stood there numb with shock.

I couldn't believe that I was being sent upstairs. Such a thing had never, ever happened to me before. I attempted to speak, but suddenly my mouth felt drier than the desert.

'Yes, you as well, Archie,' shrieked Cheryl.

I didn't exactly want to get into a face-to-face argument with her, as she has an intimidating air. So I decided I'd wait until Dad arrived home before I said anything else.

I lay on my bed seething with indignation. How dare she banish me upstairs. HOW DARE SHE!

Dad got back from rehearsals quite early. Cheryl was whispering away to him for ages. Finally, he came to see me. He stood in the doorway. 'I hear you and Eliza have had another difference of opinion, Archie.'

'And I'll tell you why,' I shouted, relating tonight's events, while Dad stood rubbing his face and sighing heavily. I concluded, 'In all my years, I have never been sent to my bedroom before.'

'Perhaps you should have been.' Suddenly, Cheryl was standing beside Dad in the doorway. 'Being sent to your bedroom is part of growing up, isn't it?' And she smiled as if she'd just said something highly amusing. I gave her my iciest glare. She went on in a low voice to Dad, 'Eliza's locked herself in the toilet again.'

'Why don't you just let her move in there?' I asked. But Dad gave me a look and went off with Cheryl.

A few minutes later he returned.

'She's out,' he announced.

'I'm shaking all over with relief. Before her next lock-in, perhaps you'd remind Eliza that my bedroom is out of bounds to her at all times! You do believe she committed the crime downstairs?'

'Yes, yes,' said Dad, quickly. 'But no harm's been done.'

'One unicorn has been decapitated.'

'Well, all right, but it wasn't valuable, Archie.'

'It was to me.'

'I'll buy you another one.'

'Eliza should pay for it, really.'

'Come on, Archie, she's a nine-year-old girl in a strange house. It can't be easy for her.'

It seemed to me it was very easy for her. She was treated like some VIP child.

Dad sat down on my bed. 'You know, for a long while when I was growing up, it was just me and my mum. And when my cousin came to stay I found her so irritating at first. But in the end it was good and we—'

'Eliza's not my cousin,' I interrupted.

'Yes, all right.' Dad stood up. 'Now, let's try really hard and have a good evening. Do you think you can do that?'

He was talking to me now as if I were a child myself. I didn't care for that at all.

A few minutes later I found myself in Cheryl and Eliza's room. They wander into my room whenever they feel like it, so why shouldn't I do the same?

On one shelf Cheryl's got a bottle of her breath-crushing perfume. It's absolutely massive. A genie could live in it. Suddenly I had an urge to smash that bottle into tiny pieces. Of course I didn't, I'm far too sensible. For a moment or two, though, I was sorely tempted.

This shows how much tonight's events have disturbed my mental balance.

10.20 p.m.
Just been woken up by Cheryl talking downstairs. She was going on about someone having difficulty making friends at school. I assumed she was referring to Eliza but then I heard, 'It's so easily done, and I'm not criticizing you at all, but you have allowed him to rule the roost and show off all the time.' She was talking about ME! Well, how dare she accuse me of ruling the roost. As you know, I never show off. There may be moments when I exhibit an understanding of life which is pretty

awesome for a juvenile. But that's a completely different thing, isn't it?

I waited for Dad to jump in and defend me. He never uttered a word. Instead she started going on again. Only she was whispering (hissing, really) so it was hard to make out what she was saying. But even upstairs I could feel the knives. What pained me most, though, was Dad's silence. Why didn't he argue with her?

11.30 p.m.
Still awake. Do you ever feel your life is just one thing after another coming at you? WHACK, WHACK, WHACK. If you ever have, then you'll know exactly how I'm feeling right now.

FRIDAY FEBRUARY 27TH
7.00 p.m.
Someone burped extremely loudly in Mr Tinkler's lesson today. It was a boy called Tony Davis, who comes up and burps right in my face sometimes. He thinks it's so hilarious.

But Mr Tinkler immediately accused Miranda Jones of doing it. I now have some appreciation of what it is like to be unjustly accused and for a few moments felt an odd kinship with her.

7.30 p.m.
I keep listening out for the sounds of packing from Cheryl and Eliza's room. Haven't heard anything yet.

8.00 p.m.
Dad has just breezed into my bedroom and said, 'Oh, just to let you know, Cheryl and Eliza will be staying with us a bit longer.'

For a moment my face went all rigid with total horror. Then I burst out, 'How much longer?'

'Keep your voice down,' said Dad. 'They'll hear you.'

Struggling to control my dark despair, I asked, 'Please tell me exactly how much longer will they be in our house?'

'We don't know yet,' replied Dad, in a tight voice. Then he yawned. 'Sorry,' he apologised. 'It's really frantic at the studio . . . and next week I'm filming every day.'

'That's really good to know,' I said, smiling at him. And for a brief moment my problems were forgotten. But as soon as Dad left I remembered them all again.

If only I knew how much longer Cheryl

and Eliza would be inflicted on me. What about if they never left? What about if they stayed here for good? Was that Cheryl's secret plan all along?

I'm giving myself the creeps now. So I'd better stop.

SATURDAY FEBRUARY 28TH

Asked Dad if he'd booked me a tutor yet. He replied, rather curtly, that he hadn't. 'If you're worried about the cost you could always make him or her my birthday present. And I wouldn't ask for anything else.'

'It's not the cost,' said Dad.

I looked at him questioningly.

'Archie, I wouldn't be happy with you quitting school right now,' he said. 'Because you're not there just to gain information, are you? You're also finding out how to mix with other people – and that's just as valuable.'

All at once, I had the strangest feeling he was repeating something Cheryl had said to him. A cold shiver ran right through me.

SUNDAY MARCH 1ST

Cheryl cooked us a Sunday meal (loads of gruesome vegetables, no chips or baked beans) and was very smarmy to me – in front of Dad. She kept asking me questions as if I were a stranger who'd just dropped in for lunch. She even – shudder, shudder – gave me a hug. I've had more affectionate punches.

Later, and without warning, she and Dad started slobbering over each other. I didn't know where to put my eyes.

Cheryl has hijacked Dad away from me, hasn't she? And for the moment there is nothing I can do about this.

I am just a toy of fate.

MONDAY MARCH 2ND

Dad's away filming until tomorrow afternoon. I told Cheryl I'd cook my own evening meal. And with quiet dignity I prepared a delicious meal of beans on toast, with slices of ham on top. I took my tray of food upstairs and left Cheryl and Eliza to it. No one has come near me since. They crash around while I sit quietly up here feeling like a stowaway in my own home.

TUESDAY MARCH 3RD

Just discovered something that's awful – but awful in a really great way. Confused?

I expect you are. So am I. In fact my head's in a total whirl.

But I've got to write this very quickly because . . . well, you'll see.

It all started this morning when the heating at school broke down and all the pupils (except for those in year eleven) were sent home. I got back at approximately nine minutes to twelve. There was an unfamiliar car in the drive and I could hear music playing loudly in the kitchen and voices from the sitting room. One I recognized, the other I didn't.

The sitting room door was slightly ajar. So I peeped inside and saw Cheryl conversing passionately with a man with large ears and a grey ponytail. Then he leaned forward and stroked her hand. I didn't need to watch anymore. This clearly wasn't a man who'd dropped in to read the meter. An air of intimacy hung over those proceedings like a poison gas.

I'd stumbled on Cheryl having an assignation with a secret boyfriend, hadn't I? How dare she turn our house into her love nest?

I quickly decided the best thing to do would be to inform Dad and let him deal with this matter. But then I hit upon a snag. I could hardly ring from the house. And I don't possess a mobile phone. So I walked bristly to the post office, outside of which are two phone boxes. But would you believe they were both out of order?

So I'm now standing outside the post office, wondering what I should do. I could try and borrow a phone from someone? I'd tell them it's an emergency – which, in a way it is. Yes, I think I will do that. I'm just plucking up the courage to ask someone.

Right, off I go.

12.55
You'll never guess who I borrowed a mobile phone from . . . Miranda.

She was handing out leaflets about the unnecessary killing of whales. She'd already doled these out at school. But I took another leaflet from her, then said, 'Could I ask you something rather cheeky?'

She raised an eyebrow.

'Might I possibly borrow your mobile phone as I have to ring my dad extremely urgently?'

Without saying a word she thrust her phone in my direction. 'That's very decent of you. Thanks,' I said.

Dad answered almost right away. 'Is everything all right, Archie?' he demanded.

'Not quite.' I didn't wish to disturb the balance of his mind by revealing all the shocking details at once. So I continued. 'The heating broke down at school so I came home early and discovered a strange man in our house.'

Dad drew his breath in with a kind of whistle. 'You've disturbed a burglar,' he cried.

'Oh no, nothing like that,' I said, hastily. And I'm not being held captive or tortured or—'

'But who is this man?' interrupted Dad.

'I don't know him at all. But Cheryl does. He's just been stroking her hand . . . and she looked to me as if she was enjoying it greatly.' I'd decided it was best not to spare Dad any of the facts.

He made a sound like a tyre bursting, then in a low, tight voice muttered, 'I'm on my way home anyway. I should be there in half an hour.'

'Excellent,' I said. 'Then you'll be able to see them for yourself. Have a good journey home. Bye.'

I handed the mobile back to Miranda who was standing beside me and listening to everything. I asked, 'How much money do I owe you for that call?'

'Two hundred and fifteen pounds,' she replied.

I laughed, realizing this was a joke and added. 'I suppose that doesn't include VAT either.'

A flicker of a smile crossed her face before she asked. 'Who's Cheryl?'

I didn't mind her asking and replied, 'She's this lady who's living with us while she waits for her new house to be ready and Dad kind of likes her—'

'But you don't,' she interrupted.

'No,' I admitted. 'And she doesn't like me either.'

'I can't imagine why,' said Miranda, which I think was another of her jokes. She went on, 'Well, I'm sure she'll be packing her bags tonight.' She returned to her leafleting.

Actually, I don't want Cheryl and Eliza to move out as quickly as that. Tomorrow would be just fine. My heart's inflating like one of those fairground balloons at the thought of Dad and me having the house to ourselves again.

More soon.

4.30 p.m.
I hung around the shops for ages. I thought Dad would wish to have a good long row with Cheryl. And I respected his need for privacy at this time.

But finally, I arrived home and noticed straight away that the strange car had gone. I bet Dad had slung him out. He can be a man of action when he needs to be.

I opened the front door. Dad rushed towards me. He gave me a sad, twisted smile. 'Cheryl is packing up all her belongings.'

So Miranda was right.

He went on, 'Cheryl's played a cruel trick on me. She pretended she liked me while having secret meetings with her ex-husband.'

'So that's who he was.'

Dad nodded grimly. 'You knew from the start Cheryl was a wrong 'un, didn't you?'

I patted his shoulder in a kindly way. 'I take no pleasure in being proved right. Now, you go and get your head down for an hour or two. You've had a bad shock. When you wake up I'll cook us something. How about beans on toast with a mug of non-herbal tea?'

'Perfect,' said Dad. 'I'm feeling better already.'

STOP!

That's what should have happened tonight – and what I really believed would occur. But now I'd better give you the rotten stinking (please excuse my language) truth, which is as follows . . .

I got back to discover Dad, Cheryl and the man with the grey ponytail as chummy as anything. And when they spotted me, all three of them burst into gales of laughter.

That man's her brother, Edwin. He'd been out of the country and she hadn't seen him for yonks. But he'd traced her here and found being mistaken for Cheryl's boyfriend so hilarious, he couldn't stop laughing about it. Neither could Cheryl, or Eliza (who heard all about it when she returned from her ballet lesson, and has been in fits of laughter ever since).

Edwin left about five minutes ago. Just as he was going I heard him say my name and the laughter erupted yet again. I put my head under two pillows. I'd rather rip my ears out than have to listen to that sound anymore.

7.00 p.m.
Dad's just been to see me. He said, 'I've apologised to Cheryl on your behalf.'

'I thought I'd made her day,' I said, adding, a bit desperately, 'Did Edwin actually produce any proof that he is her . . .?'

'Oh, come on, Archie.'

'Just a passport which you could quickly check.'

'Look, we've had enough of this nonsense. Be thankful Cheryl and Edwin have got a sense of humour.'

'When I'm the joke, they have.'

Dad frowned at me. A frown that seemed to stretch down to his feet.

We were practically arguing. Something we've never done before. I really thought we were above such behaviour.

9.00 p.m.
Just can't concentrate on my maths home-work. Tinkler will go ballistic when he sees my feeble effort tomorrow. I can only hope the heating is still broken down.

WEDNESDAY MARCH 4TH

8.45 a.m.
Woke up with a black cloud hanging over me. It followed me to school where I discovered the heating is working again.

11.30 a.m.
I've just done something really terrible. Get ready to be extremely shocked.

I was sitting in Mrs Byrne's lesson thinking of who we had next (Tinkler) and how horrible it was going to be, when I suddenly felt very sick. I asked to be excused and moved nippily to the loo, but nothing occurred, if you follow me.

I still felt sick though, but kind of restless too. So I paced up and down the corridor which was devoid of life – apart from me. And I thought, I must return to Mrs Byrne's lesson now – but I didn't.

My gaze was caught by something I'd seen many times before. In fact, I must have walked past it every single day.

The fire alarm.

I stood staring at it with keen interest. Then I gave the fire alarm a little punch. I can hear your sharp intake of breath. I'm afraid it gets much worse.

Next thing I knew I was pounding my

fist against the glass. Only it stubbornly refused to break. But, instead of giving up, I took off my shoe and whacked it against the glass in a highly determined way. Well, that did it all right. My eardrums were suddenly assaulted by a piercing wail.

I couldn't move away from it either. I was rooted to the spot with horror. Then I spied Miranda – I think she was just arriving for the day.

'Did you do that?' she demanded, breathlessly.

'I fear so,' I replied, in a voice hoarse with shock. 'Any suggestions as to what I should do now?'

'Put your shoe back on,' she said. 'And run like crazy.'

I followed both these excellent pieces of advice – and only just in time, too. Seconds later pupils came spilling out of every classroom, chattering excitedly about which lessons they were missing.

'A drab day has suddenly been cheered up for hundreds of pupils. Well done,' hissed Miranda.

The headmaster wasn't quite so enthusiastic. In fact, he yelled at us through a megaphone on the back field, about all the time we'd wasted . . . and went on to waste considerably more of it.

Mr Tinkler's lesson was completely wiped out. Hooray! And now it's lunchtime and everyone's still buzzing about the fire alarm, wondering who'd set it off. No one will ever suspect me. Still can't believe it myself.

And I know what you're asking. Whatever happened to my great maturity? I've been wondering that too. But for a few moments it just seemed to melt right away like snow in the sunshine.

4.30 p.m.
This afternoon Miranda was sent for by the headmaster. She was gone ages. Afterwards I asked her, 'Did he want to see you about the fire alarm?'

'That evil, sour, meddling secretary saw me arrive at school just before it went off. So, of course she has to trot off to old Hardened Arteries and make a big deal out of it all – but they've only got circumstantial evidence. No proof.'

'Should I give myself up?'

She put back her head and laughed, then asked me, 'Why did you do it then?'

'To miss Tinkler's lesson, I suppose. I didn't mean to . . .' I paused.

'Go on.' She was looking at me as if she was really interested.

'Well, I just had this strange urge that for a few moments completely took me over.'

'And is it the worst thing you've ever done?'

'Oh, definitely.'

'What's the second worst?'

Now I was really struggling. You name it, I haven't done it. Finally, as a kind of joke I said, 'I did leave the landing light on all night once.'

'You're just a wild and crazy guy, aren't you?' She sauntered away, then turned back. 'Has what's-her-face gone yet?'

'Cheryl?'

'Yeah.'

'No, you see, it wasn't her boyfriend at all. It was her brother.'

'Well, how were you supposed to know that?' Then she added, 'Stop looking so scared. Be proud. You've done something interesting for the first time in your life.'

That was a typical Miranda compliment – being quite rude as well. Of course, I'm not proud at all. I'm full of anguish about my lapse of maturity.

Still, at least I now know what it's like to

break the school rules. So, I suppose I have added to my experience of life today.

THURSDAY MARCH 5TH
9.30 a.m.
The headmaster summoned the whole school for an emergency assembly. He gave us this long lecture about how disappointed he was in our behaviour this term. 'Oh, just shut up and get ready for the coffin,' muttered Miranda, who, to my surprise, was sitting next to me.

Then he went on to talk about the fire alarm going off. He said he knew who the culprit was. The breath caught in my throat. But he wanted the wrong-doer to come forward of his or her own accord this morning.

'Well, if he hadn't guessed before, he has now,' whispered Miranda afterwards. 'Look at you, sitting there like a perspiring beetroot.'

'I'm sorry,' I hissed back. 'But I'm just not used to wrongdoing. And he is quite scary.'

Miranda scoffed contemptuously. 'I've had scarier things fall out of my nose. Anyway, he's bluffing. And if you own up I'll kill you. That's a promise.'

So I didn't give myself up to justice. Still

wonder if I should have, though. And is the headmaster only bluffing? Just can't make sense of anything at the moment.

9.30 p.m.
Cheryl's completely re-organized the kitchen. I don't even recognize it now. Of course she never bothered to consult me – and Dad is raving about all the changes.

If Cheryl says, 'I do like to see clear surfaces,' one more time I will yell for five hours, non-stop. I mean, that's fine for her house, but why are all her petty little rules being inflicted on us? And just when is she vacating our premises? If I ask Dad he acts as if I've said something highly rude.

So I rang Nan and she said she'd try and find out. Later, Dad stomped into my bedroom. 'I do wish you wouldn't keep running to your nan with tales.'

'I merely updated her on current events.'

'Well, I'd rather you didn't.'

'Are you censoring my phone calls now?'

The words just slipped out. Dad started back. 'Of course I'm not . . . it just doesn't help.'

'It helps me. Anyway, you talk to Cheryl about me. I've heard you. You don't stand up for me either. You let her say all kinds of stuff . . .'

'Cheryl is merely pointing out—'

'Cheryl detests me.'

'Of course she doesn't'

'Of course she does,' I said.

Dad looked at me with a mixture of exasperation and bewilderment. 'I really don't know what's got into you these days.'

And I don't know either.

FRIDAY MARCH 6TH

At the end of school Miranda asked me. 'What are you doing tomorrow afternoon, about four o'clock?'

'Nothing in particular,' I gurgled.

'Well, meet me on the common. There's something I need to discuss with you.'

'Is it about setting off the fire alarm?' I asked.

'In a way it is,' she said. 'And in another way it isn't. See you tomorrow.'

Totally mystified now. But it's certainly given me something else to think about. In fact, right now, it's all I can think about.

Aunty Prue
Problem Solver Page
wow
Williams Terrace
London

Friday March 6th

Hey Aunty Prue,
  Yes, it's me again. I just wanted to
tell you you're not as useless as I
thought.
  You told me I should talk to Archie.
Well, I have done that - and survived.
Then, last Friday he did something
which made me see him in a whole
new light - he set off the fire alarm.
Afterwards he looked as if his head was
going to fall off with shock. And he
wanted to confess all. I talked him out

of that one. But he still keeps looking at me like a baffled spaniel.

So, yes, he is going to need a massive amount of support. But bubbling underneath his creepiness is someone who might just have potential.

And I'm going to help him.

In fact, I'm devizing a plan of action for him right now that will totally transform his personality.

Aunty Prue, you're right, you should never write people off. Instead, you should try and improve them. So that's exactly what I'm going to do.

Yours, very faithfully,

Miranda

Miranda calias, Troublemaker.

Chapter Seven

SATURDAY MARCH 7TH

Something truly extraordinary has just occurred on the common.

Here's what happened.

It was one of those very grey days and by four o'clock the sky was nearly as dark as dusk. Miranda was already there sitting on a swing. She was wearing a zipped-up combat jacket and two dogs lay sprawled out beside her. The West Highland terrier jumped up when I got near and started growling softly. But the other dog, a Labrador, merely twitched his nose.

'Well, here I am,' I said. 'Are these your dogs?'

'They certainly are. Meet Kelly,' she pointed at the Westie, 'and Sparky. They're both strays that I've adopted. And they're just brilliant.'

She sprang down from the swing and said, 'Right, down to business.' She sat down on the grass. I did too. 'You can come a bit closer. I won't attack you,' she said.

I laughed nervously. I'd never sat on the grass with a girl before and wasn't quite sure about the procedure. But I drew nearer and smiled hopefully.

'Until Wednesday morning,' she said, 'I thought you were . . .'

'The most annoying boy on the face of this planet . . . Why did you write that letter?'

'Because you were absolutely ghastly and driving everyone mad,' she said, briskly.

'Right, I see,' I replied.

'No, I don't think you do.' She leaned forward. 'All adults have one ambition: to turn us into clones of themselves. And some kids don't fight this.' Her lip curled scornfully. 'They've been warped into thinking adults are always right, so they sell out the person they could be, just to get adults to like them. The technical word for such people is 'bods'. But you already know that.'

'I certainly do,' I said bitterly. 'It's become my name.'

She looked at me curiously. 'And you don't like that.'

'I can assure you, I don't.'

A little smile flashed across her face. 'Good . . . although you are a particularly extreme case, you're not the only bod at our school. Lots of kids are secret bods.'

'But you could never be one,' I said.

She grinned at the very idea. 'Oh no . . . I realize adults are nothing special. In fact, they're just the same as us, only in much worse clothes. I see through them, so they label me a 'troublemaker'. Not that I care. I'd rather be a troublemaker than a bod any day. And you're either one or the other.'

She went on, 'I really liked the way you set off that fire alarm.'

I wasn't sure how to reply to that so I just coughed modestly.

'I'd written you off as a pure bod, but then another side of you came rushing out for the very first time. I'd say you've got a lot of untapped potential.'

'Thank you very much.'

Suddenly she was looking right at me. 'You're not very happy right now, are you?'

That gave me a start. 'No, I'm not.'

'You've been a bod all your life and where's it got you? I think it's time for you to be true to yourself – your real self – and become a troublemaker. I can help you.'

'But why would you?' I asked.

'Because, I'm actually a very helpful person . . . only no one ever realizes that. Now listen, if you come to school on Monday with the first two buttons of your shirt undone, I'll know you are interested in changing – and we will begin. If you don't, then I shan't ever bother you again.' She leaped to her feet. 'It's entirely up to you.' Then, with the dogs gambolling beside her, she strode away.

'Thank you for your interest in me,' I called after her. I wasn't sure if that sounded quite right. But she didn't turn round. So perhaps she never heard me.

My head is still fizzing from that encounter. I feel as if a great searchlight has just been beamed on to my life.

8.30 p.m.
Dad and Cheryl went out tonight. I looked at them all dressed up and suddenly remembered Miranda's words, 'Adults are just the same as us – only in much worse clothes,' and burst out laughing.

Once Dad would have grinned at me and said, 'What's so funny?' Today he gave me such an odd look (very similar, in fact, to the ones Cheryl gives me). Our closeness is dissolving away.

SUNDAY MARCH 8TH

5.00 p.m.
Sat downstairs this afternoon. Neither Dad nor I spoke for ages. The silence seemed to be made of glue. One thing Miranda said keeps whirling round in my head. 'You've been a bod all your life and where's it got you?' Still pondering the answer to that question.

9.30 p.m.
I have just realized something. I am totally worn out with being mature. I also believe it is time for a big change in my life.

That's why *I shall undo my two top buttons tomorrow*. Then I will just wait and see what happens next.

MONDAY MARCH 9TH

This morning I departed from the behaviour of a lifetime and undid my two top buttons. It felt so strange and slovenly at first, but I quickly came to terms with my decision.

Miranda was waiting at the school gate for me. She nodded approvingly. 'Well done, you have made your first important gesture against adult oppression. Now, here's a tip for you – having an umbrella means you're a loser.'

'I never knew that.'

'Well, everyone else does – so get rid of it. Also, give that scarf to the dustman.'

'Oh, I couldn't do that,' I protested. 'Nan knitted it for me.'

'And what's she got against you?'

'Nothing,' I began, then I realized that was one of her jokes.

'Well, bung it away in your deepest cupboard. It's blood-freezingly awful. I'd scrap the newspaper as well.'

She went on to say that she had another little challenge for me tomorrow. I want you to make your uniform more individual. You might wish, for instance, to wear your tie on your head.'

I couldn't stop a look of horror from crossing my face.

'Well, perhaps not that,' she said, 'but just something a bit personal that says you're not bound by adult rules. Now, don't let me down,' and with that she was gone.

Ever since I've been wondering what I could do.

TUESDAY MARCH 10TH

This morning I went to school without my umbrella and newspaper. I really didn't think I could leave my grey scarf behind. That was a part of me. But in the end I threw it in a drawer. I closed my eyes while I was doing it, though, to block out the full horror of my actions. Now Miranda would see how committed I was to being a 'non-bod'.

And then I wore my coat inside out. I thought that was pretty original of me. So did Miranda, who was waiting at the school gates. 'You have now proved that you are an individual,' she said.

I was very pleased to have proved that. Then I asked, 'So what happens next?'

'I'll be in contact again soon,' was her mysterious reply. Then she added, 'Tell no one else we're doing this. For now it's best if we keep it secret.'

I'm actually looking forward to my next assignment. And I feel happier about myself than I have for weeks. I never realized wearing your coat inside out could be so cheering.

WEDNESDAY MARCH 11TH

Mr Tinkler had to leave school early yesterday because he felt unwell. 'Let's hope it's nothing trivial,' said Miranda. Today he returned, but he still had a nasty cough. And his eyes looked very red and very tired. He gave back the maths homework. I got D– with SEE ME written in huge letters. But Mr Tinkler forgot to See Me. And I had no intention of reminding him.

This evening Eliza asked me, in a sneering way, why I'd started wearing my coat inside out. I gave her a really contemptuous look (inspired by Miranda, who is an expert at this) and said 'Now, that's a boring question' and laughed.

Being a troublemaker really increases your confidence.

THURSDAY MARCH 12TH

My first proper assignment today. Miranda hissed at me at lunchtime, 'Right, come on quickly while there are no teachers about.'

'Where are we going?'

'Tinkler's room – but hurry up.'

We hared off down that corridor. Miranda announced we were going to re-arrange Tinkler's classroom. I asked what the purpose of that was. She replied, 'Mind games, Archie.'

We pushed Tinkler's desk to the back of the room. Then we moved all the other desks too. We worked with great speed and efficiency. 'That'll unsettle him,' said Miranda.

And it did.

He stared around the classroom with his mouth hung open like a ventriloquist's dummy's. 'My desk . . . how did it get there?'

Thirty faces stared blankly at him.

Afterwards Miranda said, 'Nothing brightens up my day like a bit of chaos,' and winked at me.

FRIDAY MARCH 13TH

At breaktime today Miranda said, 'Mrs Rivers is away for history and they've got a supply teacher taking her place, so we're off.'

'*Off!*' I echoed. 'You mean, we're going to skive a lesson?'

'Not so loud – but yes, that's exactly what we're going to do.'

I gaped at her. She'd just sprung this on me. 'Thanks for the offer, but I'm not sure if I can partake today.'

'Of course you can. It'll be a breeze. It's also a vital part of your education. Just follow me.'

She led me round to the front of the school and explained that all the secretaries were having coffee now so it was a good time to make our bid for freedom. She said I could go first and urged me to be confident and relaxed. She added, 'If anyone stops you, just say you've got exploding diarrhoea.'

'What!' I laughed.

'No, honestly, people can't move away from you fast enough when you tell them that.'

So, armed with those two words I tottered forward.

'Stop, stop,' hissed Miranda. 'You're walking like a zombie. Here, watch me.'

She sauntered out of that gate just oozing confidence. I knew I was watching a real professional. Then it was my turn again.

I had a bit of a panic attack at first. But finally I charged forward with my head down, rather as if I were attempting to score a try in rugby.

Miranda said afterwards, 'We'll practise that.'

We walked down to the little parade of shops, my stomach twisting with nerves. I noticed a couple of women staring at us. 'Don't make eye contact with the old crows,' instructed Miranda. 'Just keep looking straight ahead.'

That's harder than it sounds. Also, cars kept swishing past and I was sure the drivers could read the guilt on my back.

When we got to the bus shelter – which was to be our hideaway – I started breathing dead quickly. 'Look at you,' said Miranda, scornfully.

'It is my first time,' I gasped.

'Thirteen years old and never skived a lesson before,' said Miranda, rolling her eyes.

'Not quite thirteen,' I spluttered.

'Well, you've done it now . . . Actually, I think pupils should always be allowed to dip in and out of school when they feel like it. It should be their right. After all, we're not prisoners or anything. Our only crime is that we're young.'

Then she went off to buy us some chocolate. We sat in the shelter munching away while she quizzed me about my home life.

'You know what you should do with Cheryl, don't you? Play mind games with her. Put her perfume bottle in the fridge, then deny all knowledge and tell her she's going mad.'

She went on, 'Your big problem is thinking you've got to be all pally with adults. Arguing with them is natural. I mean, I argue with my mum just about every single day.'

'Really!'

'Oh yeah, it's usually dead stupid things. Well, yesterday I left a towel on the bathroom floor and she acted as if it was the end of the world. She went on and on about it too. In the end I said, 'Look, Mum, tell me something new or don't talk to me at all.'

On the way back Miranda warned, 'That minute of walking in through the gates again is actually the most dangerous of all. But you know what to say.'

'Exploding diarrhoea.'

'As an extra insurance, have this.' She handed me a scrap of paper. 'People hardly ever stop you if you've got a bit of paper in your hand – especially if you hold it in the right way.' And Miranda quickly taught me how to do this.

As I was walking through the gates the caretaker came towards me. My knees buckled – but only briefly. Then I waved my scrap of paper, exactly as I'd been instructed. The caretaker gave me a quick glance. The words 'exploding diarrhoea' were forming on my lips. But he strolled on past me.

I'd done it! I was so chuffed. So was Miranda. She said, 'You're nowhere near as bad as I thought you'd be.'

I feel I've learnt so much today.

SATURDAY MARCH 14TH

4.00 p.m.

Miranda was shocked when I told her I didn't have a mobile phone. She said I was living in prehistoric times, technology-wise. So this afternoon I took some money out of my savings account and purchased one.

Called Miranda and told her. I also thanked her for teaching me how to skive yesterday.

A true milestone in my life.

6.30 p.m.
Just had a long chat with Nan on my new mobile. I wore my scarf all the time I was talking to her. She was ages knitting it and I still feel bad about the way it's been relegated to the back of the cupboard.

It's Nan's birthday today. And she wasn't at all happy about that. 'I'm galloping towards old age now, Archie.' But my card and bath salts cheered her up. Also, I'd sent her some flowers, which she says are now in a vase on a table beside a large photograph of my mum and me.

She wants to see me soon. I thought I'd better prepare her so I said, 'Well, be ready for some changes.'

'Have you shot up, love?' she asked.

I decided this wasn't the right moment to tell her I was turning into a committed troublemaker. So I just declared, 'Nan, I am no longer a bod.'

'What's a bod, love?'

'Someone who always does what they're told.'

'Well, good for you,' she said.

Chapter Eight

SUNDAY MARCH 15TH

11.30 a.m.

Freezing cold morning, with icicles hanging from the drainpipes. An icy wind seemed to be blowing through my house too.

You remember those models in the hallway? The ones that Eliza knocked over when she stole my football out of my bedroom? Well, Dad's always liked them. But right out of the blue today he announced that the shelf was looking cluttered and I should clear most of them away. I was totally astounded. Then I saw Cheryl lurking behind us and realized she was the one who'd decreed this.

'Why do you have to do everything she tells you?' I cried.

'There's no need for that,' said Dad, wearily. 'It was just a simple instruction—'

'From Cheryl,' I interrupted.

Dad let out a splutter of exasperation. Cheryl didn't say a word but her eyebrows were practically hitting the ceiling.

'Well, I'll tell you what,' I shouted. 'Why not make Cheryl really happy and pack them all away . . . and me with them.'

I stormed upstairs.

About half an hour later Dad came in with a cup of tea, which he plonked down. 'I think you owe Cheryl an apology.'

'I don't.'

'Why do you have to fight every little change Cheryl suggests?'

I merely stared at him without blinking – a look I copied from Miranda.

'We just need some give and take from you.'

'We' – why was he always saying 'we' now? I didn't reply but just went on staring at him. He suddenly cried, 'You don't run this house, you know.'

'I know I don't. Cheryl does.'

That wounded. It was meant to.

Without another word Dad left.

8.30 p.m.

Came downstairs and saw the models had all been left on the shelf. I noticed Dad slouched low in the chair, looking very dejected. I felt a pang or two of guilt.

Should I offer to put away some of the models after all as a peace offering?

I consulted Miranda.

'Are you mad?' cried Miranda. 'Do that and Cheryl's got her way. And anyway, parents love to make you feel guilty. It's what they live for. My mum tries that number on me all the time. You've really got to watch out for that.'

I was grateful for the warning and shan't attempt to resume communications with my dad tonight. I'll just go to bed early and finish *The Invisible Man* by H. G. Wells.

I wonder what my next assignment will be. Already I've got this tingly feeling of excitement.

MONDAY MARCH 16TH

Whenever Tinkler speaks, Miranda has a little smile playing about her lips. It is another of her mind games. And it seems to be working. He wasn't in a good mood at all today.

He suddenly asked Miranda why she was wearing bracelets to school. 'You know that's not allowed.'

This is true. But every day since I've been here Miranda has worn a bracelet on each arm and no teacher has ever challenged her about this before.

Even she was a bit shocked. 'They're not affecting my education,' she said. 'So what's the problem?'

'If you wear them tomorrow I shall confiscate them,' he cried.

Afterwards Miranda said, 'Why are adults always trying to impose silly, petty rules on us. When I grow up I'm going to open a graffiti park. And people can do graffiti – which is really cool anyway – wherever they want and there'll be no stupid rules about anything at all . . .'

She went ranting on for ages.

Finally, I asked, 'Will you wear the bracelets tomorrow?'

'Of course I will . . . Tinkler hasn't given me one reason why I shouldn't.'

'Well,' I suggested. 'Why not wear them to school – but take them off when we have Tinkler?'

'I shall do nothing of the sort,' she retorted, hotly.

She is recklessly brave.

TUESDAY MARCH 17TH

6.00 p.m.

Miranda came to school jangling defiantly and ready for combat. We had Mr Tinkler first. Everyone quickly took their seats.

Tinkler rushed in and started cleaning the blackboard really energetically. It was like watching someone doing press-ups before a big match.

Then he faced us, moving his head from side to side just as boxers do when they're about to enter the ring. Finally, he looked at Miranda, and pointed a trembly finger at her bracelets. 'What did I tell you yesterday?'

'Remind me,' she said, with a cheeky smile.

'I told you that if you wore those bracelets to school again they would be confiscated.'

'So you did,' murmured Miranda. 'But I don't know why. What harm are they doing you? They're just two innocent bracelets.'

'I'm not debating that matter with you,' cried Mr Tinkler. 'Give me those bracelets now.'

'But I really don't think they'll suit you,' purred Miranda.

There were a couple of smothered giggles, which were quickly silenced by Mr Tinkler's heavy glare. 'You can either hand me those bracelets or go and see the headmaster, who is in complete agreement with me on this matter and will remove them himself. Which is it to be?'

There was a long pause, during which the only sound was Mr Tinkler sucking his moustache. Then, very slowly, Miranda started removing her first bracelet. There were gasps of disappointment. The class had been expecting more fireworks from her.

'I shall confiscate these bracelets for one week,' said Tinkler, locking them in the drawer in his desk. Miranda didn't say a word, but she had an odd gleam in her eyes. Later she told me (and only me) her plan.

'I shall sneak back to school tonight, crack open that feeble lock – and get back my property.'

'But he'll know it's you that's taken them,' I cried.

'Of course he will,' said Miranda, 'especially when I wear my bracelets into his lesson tomorrow.'

'You'd do that?' I gasped.

'Of course I would.'

It was like a war between them – and neither could afford to lose.

Miranda went on, 'You'll come with me and be my look-out. Now, why are you looking like someone's just spit in your socks?'

'I'm not,' I replied hastily. 'I was only gulping a bit as I've never been a look-out before.'

'You'll be just fine. We've only got to sneak past a dozy caretaker.'

So I shall be meeting Miranda in about half an hour. What an action-packed life I'm leading these days.

9.00 p.m.

Something highly shaming to tell you.

I met Miranda at half past six. On the way to the school she told me why those bracelets were so special. They were friendship bracelets. I wondered who had given them to her. I even felt a little stab of jealousy.

When we reached the school a shock awaited us. It wasn't deserted as we'd expected. Instead, it was teeming with people. A meeting of the Ramblers

Association was being held in the hall.

'This is fine,' said Miranda. 'We'll walk in there very casually, looking like this is where we should be. Then we'll dart off to Tinkler's classroom. Right, follow me.'

I followed her into reception, where a woman with a clipboard and glasses on her nose was taking charge. Miranda slipped through the crowd like quicksilver. Unfortunately, I wasn't quite so nimble. And the woman with the clipboard pounced on me.

'May I help you?'

For a moment my mind went completely blank.

'This is a meeting of the Ramblers Association,' she explained.

'Yes, I know.' Then I added, 'I'm looking for my nan. She left her purse behind.'

'I'll see she gets it,' said the woman, stretching out her hand for the imaginary purse. 'What's her name?'

'It's all right. I see her,' I cried, rushing over to a lady with snow-white hair. The woman with the clipboard was still watching me, so I thought I'd better say something to my 'nan'.

'Hello, there,' I said, with a friendly smile. 'How are you?'

'I'm very well,' she replied, looking rather startled.

'Been rambling long?' I asked.

'About twenty-five years.'

'Oh, excellent, excellent.' Suddenly the woman with the clipboard was distracted, so I said hastily, 'Well, keep on rambling, won't you? Bye.'

I dashed over to the classrooms. Miranda loomed up out of the shadows. 'Where on earth have you been?'

'Got stopped by someone . . . but it's all right now.'

'Now, if you see anyone coming, whistle,' she instructed.

'There's just one slight problem with that,' I explained. 'I can't whistle.'

'I don't believe it,' she cried, then muttered something about 'working with amateurs'.

'I can do bird cries, though,' I said, eagerly. 'My speciality is the warning call of the corncrake. My nan's friends said it was remarkably accurate. Do you want a quick demonstration?'

'Amazingly, I don't. Anyway, I'll be dead quick, so I should be all right.'

Only she wasn't. In fact, she'd hardly set off when a familiar figure came striding towards me: Mr Tinkler.

I couldn't believe it. What on earth was he doing here? I cleared my throat and began my impression of an extremely worried corncrake. Only I was badly out of practice. And it was nowhere near as loud as I'd hoped. Mr Tinkler charged past me, and I quickly had another go. I got considerably more volume with my corncrake impression this time. In fact, that woman with the clipboard started to look puzzled.

Had Miranda picked up my warning? It was just agony waiting to find out. But worse was to follow. Suddenly I saw Mr Tinkler march back up the corridor with Miranda half-running beside him. Miranda was saying 'I just want to GO HOME!' She shouted the last two words so I guessed that was a kind of message for me.

I departed with a very heavy heart.

I'd been a total flop as a look-out and, as a result, Miranda had been captured. And I don't know what's happened to her, either. I've tried ringing her on her mobile, but she's not answering. And I just feel so bad about it all.

9.30 p.m.

Miranda's called me at last. She didn't hear any of my bird calls and was just clicking the lock open with her nail file, when Tinkler appeared.

He said he'd caught her in the 'act of theft', (though, as Miranda said, how can you steal something which already belongs to you?) and taken her off to the caretaker's office. He also rang her parents. They had to come and collect her.

'Tinkler's going to make such a big deal out of this,' said Miranda.

'I'm really, really sorry.'

'Oh, don't be,' said Miranda. 'It's not your fault. I should have been suspicious when I saw his classroom door was open and the light was still on. But can you believe he was still working at that time of night? I mean, what a bod.'

'Can adults be bods too?' I cried.

'He can.'

'So what's going to happen now?' I asked.

'Oh, it'll all just blow over,' said Miranda.

But I'm not so sure.

WEDNESDAY MARCH 18TH

12.45 p.m.

Breaking news:

Miranda's been suspended from school for one whole week. The headmaster sent for her just after the first lesson had started. And she never came back. Rumours have been racing round. But only I know the truth because she rang me on my mobile.

And she hasn't just been suspended for what happened last night. It's also for setting off the fire alarm.

'Well, the headmaster kept going on and on about it, so I thought, oh, why not throw that one in as well?'

'But I can't let you take the blame for me,' I protested.

'I'm merely adding it to my long list of crimes.'

'No, it's unjust. I'm going to see the headmaster now.'

'Don't you dare,' she growled. 'He'll think that's dead suspicious, two of us owning up to it. No, leave it, everything's going to be just fine . . . trust me, I'm a troublemaker.'

I laughed at that. But I also feel greatly humbled by Miranda's plucky behaviour. One day I shall certainly repay her.

4.00 p.m.

Just had what I can only describe as an out of body experience. It was the weirdest thing ever.

It happened at the end of school. All the pupils who'd taken part in the talent assemblies were excused lessons to have their picture taken. This would be sent to the local paper, who were running a feature on us next Monday.

And Tinkler, the school's photography expert, was taking the picture. He'd set up the automatic equipment so that he could push his unpleasing countenance into the line-up as well. And he was ages and ages doing this.

Finally he came and plonked himself right next to me. I remember him telling everyone to keep their shoulders back. Then, just as if it were being pulled by invisible strings, my left hand began rising. It hovered in the air. And, when the flash exploded, two of my fingers sprang above Tinkler's head and made a very rude gesture indeed.

Mr Tinkler was too intent on checking that the flash had gone off, to see what my fingers were up to. But everyone else had noticed all right. There were shocked and delighted giggles all round.

Tinkler muttered to me, 'I don't know what's got into them today.'

He would when he saw the picture. I was really shocked at myself. I've never done anything like that before. But, like I said, it didn't feel quite real somehow. I seemed to be just watching it happen.

Everyone was buzzing about it afterwards. And as one boy cheerfully informed me, 'Tinkler's going to blow your head off tomorrow.'

I'll stop here as I'm feeling a trifle weak.

7.00 p.m.
Told Miranda what I'd done. Afterwards she just made a strange choking sound.

'Are you all right?' I asked.

'I think I'm going to die of pride,' she replied.

That really cheered me up. Later, though, I said, 'I think tomorrow is going to be pretty horrible . . . I might even be suspended, mightn't I?'

'Archie,' she replied. 'Welcome to my world.'

5.00 p.m.

I arrived at school quivering like a blanc-mange. In registration I sat waiting for a call to see Tinkler. In my head I was already picturing the scene. His eyes would be cold with fury and he'd shout quite a lot. Afterwards, I'd be sent to the headmaster.

But, in fact, nothing happened all day. I guess Tinkler can't have developed the picture yet. To be honest, I'd rather have got my punishment over with. Waiting for something ghastly to happen is sheer torture.

But what I did yesterday has certainly sent my popularity soaring. I've been patted on the back all day – and at lunchtime I was invited, for the first time, to play football.

It's crazy, really. Whenever I've tried to improve the quality of people's lives – such as with my litter patrol – I've been mocked and sneered at. But make one rude gesture, and you receive the thanks of the nation.

8.00 p.m.

Miranda's just called. She'd been

expecting a long lecture from her mum about how she'd let the family down, yet again. Instead, her mum just said, 'We know you're going through a restless phase. We hope this time at home will help you to calm down and focus on your goals.'

'But that's good, isn't it?'

'No, it's not,' cried Miranda, 'because my mum's acting so weird I'm seriously freaked out now.'

9.00 p.m.

Miranda has rung again. She thinks if Mrs Rivers is still away tomorrow, I should skive off again. I wasn't very keen, especially in view of the perilous situation regarding Mr Tinkler. But Miranda said, 'You can't just skive once. It needs practising, you know.'

FRIDAY MARCH 20TH

5.00 p.m.

Mrs Rivers was away today. I was really hoping she'd be back as I didn't wish to skive alone – it's much more satisfying in pairs. I was annoyed with Miranda for pushing me into this, but I didn't want to let her down either. So off I went.

And I accomplished the first part of the

mission with surprising ease. I really think Miranda would have been proud of the jaunty air I assumed when leaving school.

Then I reached the shops. I was stocking up with chocolate when I heard someone behind me who sounded as if they were gasping for air. I can do a little first aid, so I turned round to encounter . . . the headmaster. And soon he wasn't the only one to be breathing very noisily.

'Why are you out of school?' he demanded.

Two words flashed into my head, 'Exploding diarrhoea,' I cried. Well, Miranda hadn't underestimated the power of those two words. The headmaster shied away from me like an alarmed horse. I rushed on. 'I thought some chocolate might help settle my diarrhoea and stop it from exploding quite so much.'

The headmaster goggled at me for a few more moments, then told me to go outside. He gave me a lift back to school, keeping the windows wide open and giving me a number of anxious glances.

At school, he asked, 'How do you feel now?'

'Might I just visit the loo once more?' I

asked. I thought that was quite a good touch.

'All right,' he agreed. 'After that, come and wait outside my room.'

I quickly tried to gather my thoughts. Then I was ushered into the headmaster's office. The omens didn't look good. He gave me a long lecture about how I had no business leaving the school site without permission and I could be suspended, and that the suspension would go on my records. His stern words poured over me while I wondered if he'd ring home. I knew Dad wasn't there but Cheryl might be. I couldn't bear it if she came to the school. I'd rather be put in a hostel for delinquents than face that.

Then, all at once, the headmaster said to me in quite a different voice, 'Recently, your father came to see me.' That was a shocker. He carried on. 'He's worried about you, saying you haven't been yourself lately. He wondered if you had any problems at school at all.'

'No, not one,' I said, immediately.

The headmaster looked at me, then went on.

'You're a very conscientious young man, but sometimes people like yourself can put themselves under a great deal of pressure. They don't always receive the support they should from their fellow pupils. They let their high standards drop.' He gazed meaningfully at my undone top buttons and loose tie. 'They feel ill and think they can't cope, so they run away. I believe that's what you were doing today.'

He didn't wait for me to answer and went on, 'Well, next time if it all gets too much for you, talk to a teacher or come and see me. My door is always open.'

I couldn't believe how reasonable he was being about this. And I didn't get punished at all. Miranda was a little cross when I told her. 'If he'd caught me skiving he'd be bouncing off the walls. Talk about favourites.'

I reminded her that I still had Tinkler to worry about. He must have seen those pictures by now. Yet, he still hadn't done anything. He's really freaking me out.

SATURDAY MARCH 21ST
My dad's birthday. I gave him a dark blue shirt which I'd bought ages ago and some shower gel. We had quite a good conversation – just the two of us. I didn't ask him why he went to see the headmaster

(Miranda advised me to keep that information in reserve for later). Instead, we chatted about *Rivals*. Dad's first episode will be aired on April 2nd. I'm really chuffed for him.

Later Cheryl appeared with her present for Dad – a truly hideous ring. It looked as if it had come out of a Christmas cracker (perhaps it had). But it wasn't until I spoke to Miranda that I realized its true, terrible meaning.

'That means they're getting engaged,' she said. 'Or it will do, when your dad gets her one as well.'

I couldn't speak at first. Well, it's hard to utter anything when you feel as if your insides have just been torn out and scattered to the four winds.

'I bet your dad buys her a ring any day now,' said Miranda.

SUNDAY MARCH 22ND

Miranda tried to cheer me up by saying, 'When your dad marries Face-ache, I'll be waiting at the church. Only I won't be throwing confetti. No, I'll have some rocks on me.'

'Throw one for me,' I said.

Tonight, Dad told me he was going out

for a meal with Cheryl. A shine came into his aged eyes when he informed me. I had a horrible premonition that when Cheryl returned she'd have a ring on her finger too. I was so racked with horror I couldn't sleep.

In the end, I waited up for them.

When they finally got back Cheryl said, 'You waiting up for us makes me feel like a teenager again,' and chortled away at her little joke.

Still, I'm relieved to report her finger remains ringless – for now.

MONDAY MARCH 23RD

6.15 a.m.
Just had a ghastly thought. What if Tinkler didn't spot my rude gesture and sent the picture off to the local paper. Would they print it?

They just might, mightn't they?

7.30 a.m.
Just back from the newsagent. The local paper was being unpacked when I got there. I grabbed the very first copy. On page six there were four pictures featuring the talent assemblies – including one of me tap-dancing. But no group picture.

What's going on?

1.30 p.m.
Tinkler said he wanted to see me at twelve-thirty today. 'This is it,' I thought. I was so scared, my left leg started juddering all by itself . . . and wouldn't stop.

He asked me to sit down, then said, 'I've been wanting to see you about something rather serious.'

'Oh yes,' I squawked.

'I'd meant to see you last week but I'd been feeling unwell. It's about your maths. I think you have lost your way.'

He started explaining things to me. Only terror had made my brain go all sloppy. I was hopeless. He didn't get mad, though. In fact, he was extremely patient. And totally different to how he is in class.

As I was leaving he said, 'Good to see that picture of you tap-dancing in the local paper today.'

I just hung my head.

'Such a shame the group picture I took didn't come out.'

'Oh, didn't it?' I cried.

'No, I was very disappointed about that.'

I tried my best to look disappointed too,

when really I was thinking, HOORAY! HOORAY! and HOORAY again.

When I told Miranda all this she was instantly suspicious. 'I still think he's up to something.'

'Do you?'

'Oh, yes, and why is he suddenly so nice to you? No, he's plotting something all right.'

8.30 p.m.

Just had a really odd conversation on the phone with Miranda. She said, 'So, tell me about your evening.'

'Well, I got home, made myself beans on toast, ate it in my bedroom, watched some telly, read a bit more of my book . . .'

'So, really, you're just shut up in one room.'

'To be honest, I'd rather be up here. Dad's due back soon, he'll probably pop in and see me later.'

'But that isn't right,' she cried. 'You're not a lodger. That is your house. Your dad needs to be brought to his senses. Well, don't worry. I'm working out a brilliant plan.'

'Oh, thank you.'

'And it's going to change everything.

You and I are going to swap houses.'

'What!'

'I've got it all worked out. Meet me on the common at four o'clock tomorrow. I don't want to say any more on the phone. Just be there, all right?'

'Yes, OK.'

'See you then.'

I still can't figure out what she's talking about. I mean, how can she and I swap houses?

A Reply From Aunty Prue

Dear Miranda,

Thanks for your most recent letter and I am very pleased to hear you found my reply helpful. I am a little worried about one point which I wish to clear up.

I recommended that you try to talk to Archie and understand him. I DID NOT advise you to attempt to change him.

Personally, I think trying to improve people is always a bad idea.

Perhaps it's best we just try and improve ourselves.

With best wishes,

pp Aunty Prue

Aunty Prue
Problem Solver Page
WOW
Williams Terrace
London

Tuesday March 24th

Dear illegible signature, pp Aunty Prue,
   Your letter made me very angry. You
say I should have accepted Archie as
he was. But he was impossible. Ask anyone. He had to change and I'm the one
who's helping him do it. Plus, he's
having the time of his life.
   By the way, I'm also sorting out
Archie's dad. He has taken up with a
gold-digger called Cheryl and moved
her and her daughter in. Since then,
Archie's become an extra in his own
house. It's just disgraceful what's been
going on there.

So tonight, I met Archie on the common after school. Archie gave me his key and I let myself into his house. Archie stayed on the common. I gave him a bar of chocolate, so he was fine. I went upstairs to Archie's bedroom and waited for the rest of this family from Hell to arrive.

Soon I could hear the brat nattering away with the gold-digger. Neither of them came near me. Finally, the gold-digger called up, 'Archie, have you eaten tonight?'

Brilliantly impersonating Archie's tones, I replied, 'I have eaten suffi-cient, thank you.'

Around seven o'clock Archie's dad came home. He was moaning away to the gold-digger about what an exhaust-ing day's filming he'd had, but not one word was said to me.

Hours crawled by. And it was such an unhappy little room. Even the air felt stale and trapped. This wasn't a bedroom, it was a cell. I thought of Archie, stuck up here by himself every night. Some of his loneliness even melted into me. Then I got really worked up, because I just hate cruelty.

Archie's dad finally tapped on the door – at eight forty-five 'All right, Archie,' he said.

'No, I'm not all right,' I yelled back. 'And you should be ashamed of yourself.'

He charged inside, then gaped at me in total bewilderment. His eyes are identical to Archie's – pale blue and rather fluttery. 'But who are you?' he demanded.

'Let's just call me the ghost of Christmas past.'

'Where's Archie?'

'He's safe.'

'But how did you get in here?'

'Archie gave me his key. Do you know, I've been in this house since half past four.'

He was in total shock.

Then the gold-digger bustled in. 'What on earth's going on here?' she cried.

'My question, exactly,' I replied.

The squawky munchkin rushed in too. She stared at me with huge eyes. 'Why are you in this bedroom?' she asked.

'Why are you still alive?' I replied.

Shortly afterwards Archie's dad drove me to the common. 'I don't find this charade the least bit amusing, you know.'

'This charade, as you call it,' I snapped back, 'wasn't supposed to be amusing.'

That shut him up all right.

Poor Archie was freezing to death, waiting for us on the common. But it was a good evening's work - as I think you'll agree. And I'm certain things will change in Archie's house now.

Sorry this has been such a long letter. But you had no business criticizing me - as I hope you now realize. Actually, I'm a ray of blooming sunshine in Archie's life.

Hope you are feeling well.

Miranda

Miranda (alias Troublemaker)

Chapter Nine

TUESDAY MARCH 24TH

I've just spent almost five hours shivering on the common. In the end my ribs were rattling with hunger.

It was all Miranda's idea. She suggested going home in my place and seeing how long it took for my dad to notice. As you've no doubt guessed, it took him ages.

Still, I'm not sure he grasped the point of the exercise. When he turned up on the common he didn't rush over to me full of remorse for his neglectful ways. Instead, he had a face like thunder. And in the car, he said, through gritted teeth, 'Of all the stupid stunts . . . well, I just don't trust myself to speak.'

'Best keep quiet then,' I replied.

Dad gave me his worst look. And the rest of our journey was passed in silence. He told me off again when I got home. Cheryl was there too (of course). She didn't say anything, but there was a lot of eyebrow action coming from her direction. Dad made me a hot drink as I was still shivering with cold and Cheryl asked me, 'That girl who was here tonight . . . are you and she . . .?' She paused. I knew what she was asking. But I had no intention of discussing such confidential matters with her, so I just stared blankly.

'As soon as you've had your drink go straight up to bed,' said Dad.

'Oh goody,' I replied, gulping the drink down. 'Nighty nighty, everyone.'

I walked nonchalantly up the stairs. But inside I was seething with disappointment. Dad hadn't learnt a single thing from tonight's exercise. And I got frozen alive for nothing.

WEDNESDAY MARCH 25TH
9.30 p.m.
The atmosphere at home is now thick with tension. I'm constantly waiting for Dad to announce his engagement and my whole life to split wide open.

I just couldn't stay in my bedroom this evening. Instead, I slipped downstairs. They were all in the kitchen, so I sat innocently watching some telly when I suddenly noticed I was being observed – by Cheryl.

'Not doing any homework tonight?' she asked, in a snotty voice.

Well, I was just sick of her poking about in my life and murmured, 'Oh, wind your neck in.' A phrase I'd heard Miranda use.

Of course, Cheryl couldn't march off fast enough to tell Dad about the naughty thing I'd said to her, who then ordered me upstairs to write a letter of apology.

I wrote:

Dear Cheryl,
Multiple apologies for telling you to wind your neck in. That was rude of me and there's never any call for rudeness. But I'd be grateful if you would respect my privacy at all times.
Archie.

Now, I think that's a reasonably polite letter under the circumstances. But Dad hated it, made me re-write it, and also said I'm grounded until further notice.

Miranda was furious when I told her what had happened tonight. 'What did I tell you about adults? – you can't trust a single one of them. After all you've done for your dad, too. But as soon as some woman with a face like a chisel bats her eyes at him, you're totally forgotten. I bet he never even asked you why you told Cheryl to wind her neck in.'

'No.'

'Typical, not interested in hearing your side . . . Oh, I'm furious.'

She really cheered me up, actually.

THURSDAY MARCH 26TH

6.00 p.m.

After school Miranda summoned me to another meeting on the common. 'I can't bear to think of you living in such torment any longer,' she said. 'I reckon you should just go.'

'Run away, you mean,' I said.

'Oh no, running away is what you do when you're about three. No, I mean move in somewhere . . . like, with me. We've got a spare room in the attic which we use for guests.'

'But I just can't take up residence there,' I said. 'What will your family say?'

'Claire's away on a school trip to France, Dad's in America. Richie isn't worth bothering about.'

'And your mum?'

'She's still off her head. She came into my bedroom today and said, "I see your room's still in its usual state of creative disorder," and smiled about it. So I haven't a clue what she'll say. Let's do it and find out.'

'I don't know. I mean—'

'Oh, honestly,' erupted Miranda. 'That's the trouble with you. You always put obstacles in the way so you end up not doing anything. Look, do you want to come and live with me?'

'Yes, I do,' I said.

A little smile crossed her face. 'Well, stop gassing then. It's time for action.'

We've hatched a superb plan.

I shall secretly pack tonight – not everything, just life's essentials, like pants and socks and a toothbrush (not to mention my diary, of course).

More news soon.

8.30 p.m.
I'm all packed.

I have also composed a letter to my dad, which I shall post tomorrow:

153

Dear Dad – and any other interested parties,

Just to let you know I have vacated my bedroom and moved on to pastures new. I shall send you my new address shortly.

Please do not try and find me. It just isn't working out any more, so it is for the best.

Kind regards from your son.

P.S. I shall be incurring some expenses in my new existence. If you wish to make a contribution towards these, please leave the money in an envelope with my name on at the local post office. I shall pick it up from there.

P.P.S. I repeat, do not try and find me. I shall not be leading the life of a vagabond on the run. I will be going to a good home and am not in any danger.

Archie.

Afterwards I wasn't sure about that line where I said I was going to a good home – it made me sound like a puppy. But I thought it might reassure him.

9.30 p.m.
Dad's just come into my bedroom – luckily

154

I'd hidden my bags away. I expected another lecture, so I snapped my eyes shut and pretended to be asleep. But he didn't have anything to say, just stood looking at me for a while, then went away.

I hope he'll be a tiny bit miserable when he discovers I've moved on. But Cheryl will tell him it's for the best. And on this one occasion I have to agree with her. Soon I'll be no more than a distant memory for him. Actually, I already feel a bit like that. The next time I write in these pages I'll be living in a completely different place. I still can't believe that.

FRIDAY MARCH 27TH

This is being written in my new home up in the attic. Miranda thinks it's important to wait for the right moment before informing her mother that she's got a lodger. So for now, I'm a big secret. Well, that's all right. Quite exciting, in fact.

I had to wait outside Miranda's house until she gave me a signal that the coast was clear. Then I pelted inside, scrambled up the ladder and through the trapdoor at the top and into my new residence.

Here I am!

I suppose it's fairly primitive – very

ragged carpet, no heating, a camp bed and not many facilities. Although there is a light and a little window looking on to the back garden. And once I've unpacked all my stuff I know it will seem dead homely.

5.55 p.m.
A call of nature necessitated me sneaking downstairs. I bumped into Richie. He stared at me very gravely. 'Are you a burglar?' he asked.

'I can see why you might think that,' I said. 'But actually, I'm staying here as a guest of Miranda's . . . only she hasn't told your mum yet.'

'Are you living up there?' He pointed at the attic.

'That's right.'

His face lit up. 'I wanted to live up there but Mum wouldn't let me.'

'Well, you must come and visit,' I said. 'But for now, it's all very hush-hush, all right?'

He nodded eagerly. 'Have you run away?' he called after me.

'No, I've just moved out,' I whispered back. 'Bye.'

I'm pretty certain he'll keep my secret.

7.00 p.m.

Miranda's dropped in twice now. The first time she brought me up some chocolate. The next time a fluffy rug from her bedroom. 'I've always hated it,' she said. 'And now I've got a proper reason to get rid of it.'

The second time Richie insisted on accompanying her. 'You're so lucky living up here,' he said. 'How long will you stay?'

I hesitated.

'Oh, for years,' said Miranda. 'Until he leaves school anyhow.' Then she said, 'Sssh . . . Mum's finished ringing Dad. We must go.'

'When do you think you'll tell her about me?'

'Oh, in a day or two,' said Miranda. 'Maybe on Sunday afternoon. She's usually a bit dozy then. Well, dozier than usual. Anyway, make yourself at home, even though you're not.' Then she smiled. 'No, this really is your home now. I just wish you'd stop looking so blooming serious. You haven't robbed a bank or anything. You've merely changed addresses and everyone's got a right to do that.'

'Do you think my dad will have noticed I've gone yet?'

'I doubt it,' she replied, cheerfully. 'He'll be too busy slobbering over Hatchet-features. Bye.'

The attic felt extremely quiet after they'd gone – and rather cold, too. But soon Miranda will explain it all to her mum and I shall be able to move about the house in perfect freedom.

Now I shall start re-reading *The Prisoner of Zenda* by Anthony Hope, which is one of my all-time favourite books.

8.25 p.m.
I expect Cheryl will have noticed I've gone. In fact, she's probably rented out my room by now.

9.15 p.m.
The evening has turned out to be highly eventful.

Shortly after I'd completed my last entry I opened the attic door a little bit. I felt like a tortoise peeping out of its shell. I was certain everyone was downstairs. A sharp cry quickly alerted me that I was mistaken.

A lady, who I assumed was Miranda's mum, was staring up at me with consider-able concern.

'Do not be alarmed by my sudden appearance,' I said, trying to smile down at her in a reassuring way.

'What on earth are you doing up there?' she demanded, in a strangled voice.

This was a fair question and I could totally appreciate her need for more information. So I said quickly, 'Don't worry, I'm not here illegally. I'm a guest of Miranda's. My name is Archie. And it's extremely nice to meet you.'

Before she could reply, Miranda came thundering up the stairs, closely followed by Richie.

'I see you've met Archie,' Miranda said, breathlessly. 'I was about to tell you about him. He was dead miserable in his house and couldn't stay there another second. So I said he could come and live in our attic.'

'But you can't—' began her mum. Then she stopped and cried, 'This isn't the boy whose father has just rung up?'

I pricked up my ears at that.

'You said you didn't know anything about him running away, Miranda.'

'I got confused,' Miranda replied. Then she added, firmly, 'But there's no way he's going back there.'

'Come on, Mum, let him stay,' cried

159

Richie, who was fizzing with excitement about it all. 'We can afford to feed him.'

'And he won't be any trouble up there,' said Miranda. 'You'll hardly know he's there, really.'

I felt a bit like a new exotic pet that Miranda had rescued and brought home.

'You're all talking nonsense,' said Miranda's mum, shaking her head vigorously. 'It's out of the question for him to . . . Look, will you come down please?'

'Righto,' I said, clambering down the steps.

'And Miranda,' she asked, 'what were you thinking of getting this boy to hide in our attic? You've done some irresponsible things in your time, but this tops them all!'

'Well, excuse me,' cried Miranda. 'I was merely trying to help a fellow human, who's just worn out with stress and neglect. I didn't realize that was a crime in this house.'

Miranda's mum looked at her. Then all at once her voice seemed to change. 'Now, I can see you thought you were acting for the best and you meant well. I'm sure we can sort this out. But I have to ring . . .' She looked at me questioningly.

'Archie,' I prompted.

'Archie's father. He must be out of his mind with worry.'

'No, he's just out of his mind,' muttered Miranda. She whispered to me, 'Refuse to go with him. Say the only way you'll leave is if he carries you out, or gives you knockout drugs. I'm going to work on Mum again. Did you see the way she totally changed her tune? She's definitely cracking up.'

Miranda's in the kitchen now with her mum. I'm in their sitting room with a mug of tea, scribbling away until Dad . . . I hear a car now. I'd better go.

10.30 p.m.
VICTORY!

Dad rushed in shaking with fury. 'Have you any idea how much trouble you've caused tonight?' he yelled at me.

'Have you any idea,' raged Miranda, 'how completely unhappy Archie's been in that house? He just couldn't take it any more. So, he escaped here, and he's not budging. Are you, Archie?'

'No,' I said, folding my arms defiantly. 'I'm not. And by the way, a letter is on its way to you explaining all this and answering any other questions you might have—'

'But he's got nothing more to say to you tonight,' cut in Miranda. 'Have you, Archie?'

'No, I haven't,' I said and turned my back on him.

Miranda's mum intervened. 'As emotions seem to be running rather high at the moment, might I suggest Archie stays here – just for tonight. My daughter Claire is in France so Archie could have her room—'

'Well done, Mum,' cried Miranda. 'For the first time since I was born you haven't embarrassed me.'

'I'm highly grateful,' I said, turning round again.

Dad went all red and I could tell he didn't like the idea at all. But he went into a huddle with Miranda's mum and finally announced, in a tired, defeated voice, 'All right, Archie, you can stay here for tonight. But I'll be round for you first thing tomorrow.'

'I wouldn't waste your petrol,' cried Miranda.

Dad went out far more quietly than he'd arrived.

'Round one to us,' said Miranda triumphantly. 'I just love defeating adults. In fact, it's what I live for.'

'You know,' I said suddenly, 'I don't think I'll ever go back to that house.'

'I know you won't,' laughed Miranda. 'Instead, I'm stuck with you.'

SATURDAY MARCH 28TH

10.30 a.m.

Woke up early. No one else seemed to be about, so I got dressed and then had a look round Claire's room. One wall was completely covered with certificates.

'That's not all of them, you know,' said Miranda, suddenly appearing in the doorway. 'She's got tons more of them stuffed away in a drawer.' She lowered her voice to a whisper. 'She's so perfect, it's revolting,' then plonked down a cup of tea. 'Don't expect this every morning. And don't sit up here like a guest either. Roam about freely. Remember, you live here now.'

Later I had breakfast. I insisted on doing the washing up. I also told Miranda's mum about all the things I could cook. I'm sure her mouth started watering. She said to me, 'I know it's not an easy situation for you. I had a stepfather when I was thirteen. And I resented him so much at first—'

'Oh, Cheryl isn't my stepmother,' I interrupted, hastily.

'Not yet, she isn't,' cut in Miranda. 'But give her time.'

Miranda and I are taking the dogs off for a long walk now.

12.40 p.m.
When we got back Dad was waiting for me in the kitchen. 'Don't even talk to him,' hissed Miranda. 'Run upstairs.'

This was sound advice and for good measure I locked myself in the loo (inspired by you-know-who).

A few minutes later Dad was hammering on the door. 'Come on, open up, Archie. This has gone on long enough.'

Before I could reply Miranda was yelling, 'Just what do you think you're doing, shouting and banging on the door like a raving loonie. What do you think all this is doing to Archie's state of mind?'

It was great hearing Miranda standing up for me like that. I suddenly felt strangely peaceful and happy.

After a while Miranda's mum suggested she and Dad discuss the matter calmly downstairs. Well, they gulped tea and talked for a bit. Then Dad left again and Miranda's mum announced that I could stay for the weekend.

'That means for ever,' crowed Miranda. 'He's given up. We've won.' She was very pleased. So, of course, was I. But I was also a little shocked Dad hadn't put up more of a fight for me. I expect my letter – which he'd have read this morning – convinced him I meant business.

'Do you see what happens when you stand up to adults?' said Miranda triumphantly. 'You'd have gone on meekly living with Hatchet-face and getting more and more miserable if it hadn't been for me, wouldn't you?'

'I probably would,' I agreed.

'You've learned a powerful lesson today,' she declared.

I wondered, was Dad actually relieved that I'd packed my bags? I suppose his life really is much easier now. Well, that's just fine. I'd better get back to my exciting new life.

9.30 p.m.

Went into town with Miranda this afternoon. She took me to this rescue centre for animals. She washed all four of the new dogs (I helped) and then weighed them and cut their nails. She helps out there every week. When we got back I played some card games with Richie (I even let him cheat) and assisted Miranda's mum in the kitchen. Later I was invited into Miranda's bedroom or, as she calls it, 'her escape pod'.

'I should warn you, my parents think my room's a health hazard and go on about all the diseases growing in here.'

It was incredibly messy and you had to wade through clothes on the floor – but it also had an amazing collage of pictures which stretched right across one wall. I couldn't stop looking at it.

'This is brilliant,' I said.

'I know. Now, I bet you're wondering where I keep all my certificates.'

'So you've got some too,' I cried.

'Of course I haven't. That's the trouble when you've got a girl genius for a sister – everyone compares you with her. And they expect things. I guess that's why I never put my all into anything. I'm sure I'd be rubbish. But at least I don't know for certain.'

Miranda's mum looked in.

'Welcome to the rubbish mountain,' cried Miranda, defensively.

'How many cups are up here now?' asked her mum.

'Twenty-five at the last count,' replied Miranda.

Miranda's mum said, quite gently, 'Well, please bring some down soon . . . but right now, Richie would like you both to come downstairs. Archie's been talking to him about Monopoly.'

'Bad move,' murmured Miranda.

'He's found the board and wants us all to play,' said Miranda's mum.

Despite some muttering from Miranda, all four of us played – and you know what, I feel a part of this family already.

This has been a totally excellent day.

SUNDAY MARCH 29TH

11.00 a.m.

Slept late. Came downstairs to hear Miranda laughing extremely loudly. Her mum had just asked if I was her boyfriend. 'Oh no,' she said. 'He's just a refugee I'm helping. But he's not my boyfriend.' She laughed again. I didn't think the idea was *that* hilarious.

Later I questioned Miranda about boyfriends. She said that she had one all right, but he didn't live in this area.

'Did he give you those bracelets?' I asked.

She admitted that he had.

I didn't really want to know any more. But I'm glad she and I know where we stand on this issue. It's cleared things up. Not that it ever crossed my mind that I was her boyfriend.

2.30 p.m.

Just finished a very tasty lunch. I wanted Miranda's mum to know that money would be forthcoming to pay for my keep. So I explained to her that I'd asked my dad to leave rent money in an envelope at the post office. I said, 'I'll make sure every penny goes straight to you.' She seemed impressed by my offer and said I could call her Julia, if I liked.

I had a brief phone call from my dad this afternoon. He asked if I wanted to go home. I replied most emphatically that I did not. I added, 'My real home is here now.' Dad did not say much after that, just asked to speak to Julia.

9.00 p.m.

I've written a note to Nan letting her know about my change of address. I told her she wasn't to worry as I was totally safe and eating extremely well.

I hope I can stay with her soon. Maybe over Easter. That isn't to say I'm not having the time of my life here. I am. But over the holiday season things might get rather more crowded when Miranda's dad and the 'girl genius' (as Miranda calls her) return. Plus, I haven't seen Nan for ages and ages.

Chapter Ten

MONDAY MARCH 30TH

5.00 p.m.

Got up very early. Julia came downstairs to be greeted by the smell of frying bacon and freshly brewed coffee. She was stunned. Miranda said later that I was showing off. But I just wanted to say thank you.

When Miranda and I walked to school together we caused something of a sensation. You know what schools are like for gossip. Everyone seemed really shocked that I'd moved into her house.

'I thought you couldn't stand him,' one girl said to Miranda.

'He's improved vastly since then,' she replied, 'mainly because of my influence.'

She explained how she'd rescued me, while I stood beside her grinning self-consciously and feeling like one of those puppies she'd washed on Saturday afternoon.

Tinkler gave Miranda her bracelets back today, but she didn't look very pleased, just muttered, 'About time'.

I had another extra maths lesson with him at lunchtime. Afterwards I told Miranda how different he was on his own – really helpful and patient. 'Well, I'm planning another strike in his lesson and this time you'd better not let me down,' was her only reply.

6.00 p.m.
Miranda's just told me my dad came round when I was at school today. She thinks it was to talk terms with her mum. She believes a deal has now been struck which is excellent news.

TUESDAY MARCH 31ST
Today, the headmaster came up and asked me how I was. We talked for just a couple of minutes, but Miranda was furious. 'You've got to stop crawling to people like him. It's a very bad habit.'

'I wasn't crawling,' I retorted. 'He was just enquiring about the state of my health and . . .' I hesitated before telling her the next bit, 'to ask if I'd care to perform another tap-dancing demonstration in assembly.'

'Over my dead body,' she exploded. 'You're not his little performing monkey.'

Actually, I had already declined. But I did resent Miranda's bossiness on this matter.

This evening Nan rang up. She sounded dead worried. But I did my best to reassure her – and I think I succeeded.

WEDNESDAY APRIL 1ST
5.30 p.m.
Written in extreme haste.

When I got back from school today Julia was waiting for me. She wanted to talk to me on my own. She said that Dad was waiting at his house (you'll notice I don't call it my house any more) to talk to me. Julia thought it was important I saw him.

'Trying to get rid of me, are you?' I joked. 'And before you've tasted my banana surprise, too.' I'd been planning to prepare that for everyone tonight.

Julia replied, 'No, Archie, I've really

172

enjoyed having you visit and if things don't work out, you can come right back here.'

'Are you sure you mean that?' cried Miranda, suddenly barging in. 'I know what you adults are like for saying one thing and doing the total opposite.'

But Julia repeated her offer to me – and I believe her. Miranda sort of does too. She also offered to come with me and looked disappointed when I said this might be better on my own.

I don't know what Dad's going to ... Sorry, Julia's calling me. No more time.

10.30 p.m.
The last time I wrote I was just off to see Dad. Well, he was waiting in the doorway for me. He started acting a bit hyper – a sure sign he was nervous.

'Come in, Archie. Now, can I get you anything, a cup of tea, piece of cake, a sandwich?'

'Nothing, thanks,' I said, firmly. I took a quick look around. The house was very clean. I sneaked a look inside the fridge: it was stocked full of vegetables and Cheryl's favourite foods. I felt as if I'd been away for five months – not five days. Dad was acting that way too, treating me like a visitor.

'Well, come on, sit down on the sofa. That's brilliant. So, how are you?'

'I'm in excellent health, thank you.'

I wondered where Cheryl and Eliza were. Had they been sent out for an hour or two, or were they crouched together upstairs, eavesdropping on this conversation?

As if reading my mind, Dad said, 'By the way, Cheryl and Eliza have gone.'

'Gone!' My heart turned two somersaults.

'They moved out last night, they're staying with some other friends now.'

'I bet they were angry,' I said.

'They were annoyed they still couldn't move into their new house. They have been messed about so much lately. But they understood that they couldn't stay here any longer. This has been a little experiment that hasn't quite worked out. But anyway, we've all learnt from the experience. I know I have. And now . . .' He smiled at me expectantly. But I didn't say a word. I was too busy thinking.

Dad sprang to his feet. 'At least let me make you a welcome back cup of tea. I'll have one too.'

He dashed off to the kitchen, while I just sat there in a dazed sort of way. Then my mobile rang.

'So what's happening?' Miranda sounded anxious. I briefly explained the situation.

'But has he totally dumped Hatchet-face and the offspring from Hell?'

'I don't know.'

She made an impatient, clucking noise. 'Well, is he still wearing the ring?'

I had to think about this. 'Yes, I believe he is,' I said at last.

'Well, then he hasn't finished with her.'

'Not necessarily, he just might like the ring . . .'

'Rubbish,' she shrieked down my ear. 'Look, you're in a very strong position right now. But you've got to make the most of it. So tell him the only way you'll stay is if she's out of his life for good.'

'Oh, right,' I said, uncertainly.

'If you don't do that, Cheryl will just let things settle down for a couple of days and then she'll be back . . . even more deadly than before. So listen carefully. You ask your dad: "Have you and Cheryl broken up?" If he says "No" you get to your feet at once and leave. Got that?'

'Yes,' I said.

'Remember Archie, trust no one—'

'Except a troublemaker,' I interrupted.

She laughed. 'Don't you forget it.'

Her words were still roaring in my head when Dad returned with a tray of tea and biscuits. And I just blurted out, 'Have you and Cheryl broken up, then?'

He started. 'No . . . no, we're still good friends and still seeing each other.'

I immediately rose to my feet.

'Now look, you mustn't blame Cheryl for any of this. It was my fault. I put her in an impossible situation.'

'And me,' I cried at him. 'You put me in an impossible situation too.'

'Yes, yes, I know that. But Cheryl really did think she was helping. I asked her to help, in fact. As I was away such a lot I handed things over to her. I shouldn't have done that . . . but that's behind us. It'll be totally different with Cheryl—'

'You say that now,' I interrupted. 'But what other assurances can you give me?'

He hesitated. 'Well I . . .' he stuttered.

I didn't wait for him to say anything else. Instead, I marched into the hall. 'I'll walk back to Miranda's,' I said. 'Thanks for the update. Good night.'

'No, Archie,' Dad cried. 'Don't go like this, please.'

I stopped. And then I noticed something unbelievable. All my models on that shelf in the hall had gone. Not a single one was left.

'Where are they?' I gasped, pointing.

'I meant to mention that. We just thought while you were away, they might be safer packed away upstairs in your bedroom—'

'So there's nothing of me in this house now,' I blazed at him. 'Not one single thing.' I tore outside, just as Miranda's mum and Miranda were pulling up in the car.

'I want to get away from here right now,' I cried. And after Miranda's mum had spoken very briefly to my dad, that's exactly what happened.

Later I told Miranda what I've been telling you. She sighed indignantly, throughout, then gave my hand a quick squeeze. 'Your dad's the pits. Best to just forget about him from now on.'

I suppose she's right.

But how can you just forget about your dad?

THURSDAY APRIL 2ND

Another strike in Tinkler's lesson, organized, of course, by Miranda. This time we all refused to speak to him. Whenever he asked us a question we just shrugged our shoulders or shook our heads.

Miranda was hoping he'd get dead mad and it'd be really funny. But he didn't — and it wasn't. Instead, he just said, 'All right, if you wish to remain silent, that's fine with me. We shall just press on with more work.'

Because of a staff meeting Tinkler had to switch my extra maths lesson to after school. I wasn't exactly looking forward to it. But there were a couple of minutes when I nearly understood maths. If only he were like this in class.

I was packing away when he said, 'I understand you are staying with Miranda Jones now.' I confirmed this was the case. I could tell the news didn't exactly put a spring in his step.

He leaned forward and whispered, as if imparting a great secret, 'Don't throw away everything you've achieved for a few moments of easy popularity . . . I happen to think you're worth more than that.'

He said those last words really slowly and significantly. And right then I knew something. It shot through my head, and gave me quite a shock. And I had to say something about it right away. In fact, the words just fell out of me.

'Excuse me asking, but that picture of us you took for the local paper – it did come out, didn't it?'

'Yes it did,' said Tinkler, quietly.

'So you saw what I did,' I said, in an even quieter voice. I was blushing with shame as well. 'But you never told anyone. You even pretended the picture hadn't come out. Why did you do that, sir?'

Mr Tinkler suddenly looked right at me. 'Because that wasn't the real you. You acted that way because you'd temporarily lost your bearings.'

'No,' I began. But then I decided this wasn't the moment to explain that I had a whole new personality now. So I just said, 'Thank you for what you did. I am in your debt,' then added, quickly, 'About Miranda Jones. You judged her right away. Never gave her a chance. And if you see her as bad, well, she might as well be bad, mightn't she?'

Mr Tinkler shot to his feet. 'Thank you,' he said, in a this-conversation-is-over-now tone of voice, his face as blank as a stone.

I left without another word.

Later I talked to Miranda about it all.

'Tinkler destroyed that picture for his own reasons,' she snapped. 'He was afraid it would look as if he was really unpopular ... which he is. And the strike goes on again tomorrow.'

'But I don't see the point of that,' I argued. 'He'll only set us extra work again.'

'It looks to me,' said Miranda, sternly, 'as if you're having a major relapse, getting all pally with Tinkler—'

'No,' I cried.

'In fact, you're sinking right back into your bad old ways.'

'You can't say that.'

'I just have.' And with that she swept off.

She was in a really foul mood. We haven't spoken since.

8.30 p.m.

I've just watched Dad make his TV debut on *Rivals*. I thought I would burst with pride. He was sensationally superb. I think he stole every scene he was in.

It was kind of odd watching Dad on screen whilst sitting with Julia and Richie (Miranda remained in her bedroom). Richie kept bouncing about saying, 'So that's really your dad?'

Afterwards Julia asked if I wanted to ring Dad. And I did, very badly. I called him up but the phone was engaged. I thought, I bet that's Cheryl he's talking to, and didn't ring back again.

10.15 p.m.
Miranda's just told me why she's been in such a foul mood. When she got in from school she heard her mum talking on the phone – and Julia kept mentioning Miranda's name. So Miranda had no choice but to pick up the other extension and find out more.

It turned out that Julia was talking to a child tamer. I'd never heard of such people but according to Miranda they're the latest phenomenon. 'Of course the entire conversation was about me' said Miranda. 'And the tamer kept gushing things like, "You must never use negative words to Miranda and find something worth praising in everything Miranda does," as if I were some kind of dangerous freak.'

'You're not a freak,' I replied at once. 'But I'd say you can be pretty dangerous.'

Miranda smiled briefly at that.

'What really gets to me,' she went on 'is that I actually thought Mum was starting to like me. I should have realized . . . you can't trust a single adult.'

FRIDAY APRIL 3RD

2.30 p.m.

My class refused to hold another strike in Mr Tinkler's class. They said they had to work harder when they were striking than on a normal day. Miranda argued, 'What does that matter when a principle is involved?' But no one agreed with her. I was secretly very relieved (and that is a big secret).

I had a wild hope that Tinkler might apologise to Miranda for his unfair treatment of her. Nothing of the sort occurred, but he did say, 'Thank you, Miranda,' on receiving her exercise book. Afterwards Miranda pretended she hadn't noticed. But she had.

Could this be the first sign of a thaw in relations between them?

5.00 p.m.

You won't believe who I've just seen: Nan! She was waiting at Miranda's house for me. It was a magic surprise. 'Missed your nan, have you?' she asked.

'Have I?' I cried, running over to her.

She said I'd got taller but thinner in the face. She had messages from all her friends – who are my friends too. They want to see me again soon. I've always been a big hit with the senior citizens.

Nan and I are going out for a meal now. Miranda whispered to me to be extremely careful. 'She could be working for your dad. Remember, you will only return when your terms are met in full – which they never will be. Your home is here now, isn't it?'

I agreed that it was.

Back soon.

10.30 p.m.
Lots to report.

First of all, Nan and I had a really enjoyable meal together. I was so happy to be in her company again. But over the chocolate mousse our conversation took a more serious turn.

Nan told me that she'd arrived in town earlier this afternoon to have a long chat with my dad. 'What I'm going to say now, he knows about, so I'm not going behind his back. But I can keep silent no longer. I'm just furious about the way you've been treated by him and his lady friend. And I want you to come back with me tomorrow.'

'Tomorrow!' I gasped.

'Yes, that's right. We'll have Easter together and you can return to your old school . . . and well, just carry on as before.'

'Only Dad won't be there?'

'No, he won't,' she said, firmly. 'He can come and see you whenever you wish. This is up to you. But I'd love you to come back with me so much.' Her face went a bit wobbly. So did mine.

The next thing I knew I'd agreed to live at Nan's house again. Yes, I know I'd promised Miranda only an hour earlier to go on living with her and I still wanted to do that too.

Confused! Well, you just wait.

Anyway, Nan said we'd better go and tell Dad what I'd decided. My stomach tightened. 'I expect he'll be relieved to have me off his hands.'

'Oh no, he won't feel that,' murmured Nan.

The taxi pulled up at my old home. Dad loomed up out of the darkness. He'd obviously been watching for us.

'You've been a long time,' said Dad.

'No we haven't,' said Nan, rather snappily.

Inside, the first thing I noticed was that all my models were back on the shelf in the hall. The second was the amount of food set out in the sitting room. There were plates of cakes, biscuits, chocolate, crisps . . . enough for a small party.

'We have just eaten, you know,' said Nan.

'Yes, of course you have.' Dad's face fell. 'Well, just in case you're feeling a bit peckish later.'

'Now,' said Nan, in a business-like way. 'I explained to Archie that he could, if he wished, come and stay with me and that is what he wants to do, isn't it, Archie?' She looked at me.

'Yes, that's right,' I said, feeling more muddled than ever.

'So I suggest Archie comes back here tomorrow morning, packs up his things, then we'll get a train . . .' she talked on. Dad's eyes were all wide and staring. He looked like someone who'd been suddenly woken up in the middle of the night.

'Well, I'll go back with Archie now,' said

Nan, 'and explain things to Mrs Jones and Miranda. I've already ordered a taxi.' And, right on cue, there was a ring on the doorbell.

Nan left tactfully, giving Dad and me a moment on our own. He insisted on packing up some of the food for me. He was ages doing it. I longed to help him but resisted the urge. 'Well, you can eat it at your leisure,' he said.

'Thank you,' I replied.

'And Archie, I'm so very sorry for making a complete mess of everything. I don't blame you going off with your nan.' His voice began to shake. 'It's all I deserve.' He stretched out a hand to me. 'I'll be along to see you at your nan's very soon. Take good care of yourself, won't you?'

'And you,' I said. 'By the way, you were totally excellent in *Rivals* yesterday and I shall be . . .' now my voice began to shake too, 'following your career with great interest.'

After that, I tore out of the house and into the taxi. It set off right away. I sat there breathing very hard, until I announced, 'Sorry, we've got to stop. I've forgotten something.'

Actually, I hadn't done anything of the

kind, I just couldn't leave yet. I pelted back up the drive. Dad was still standing there, looking totally defeated. Then he saw me and neither of us said a word. We just clung on to each other for ages. We walked back into the house together, and would you believe, I'm going back to live with him again.

I bet you're totally mixed up now, aren't you? Sorry to do that to you. But I've been in a torrent of confusion for days. Yet I really think I've made the right decision *at last*.

Nan looked very disappointed when I told her but just said, 'If that's what you want, love, I'll support you.'

Miranda was much, much angrier. She stomped about my room, proclaiming, 'But you don't know about Cheryl. Is he still seeing her?'

'I didn't ask him.'

'What!' she shrieked.

'I just think it will be all right now.'

Miranda looked at me, her eyes suddenly very dark. 'And I just think your brain's fallen out.' Then, without another word she marched off.

Chapter Eleven

SATURDAY APRIL 4TH

12.30 p.m.

Right after breakfast I packed up all my stuff from Miranda's house. Julia and Richie helped. Miranda stayed in her bedroom. In the end, I knocked on her door and went in. She was sitting on the bed, with her arms wrapped around herself, staring intently out of the window.

'Looking at anything interesting?' I asked, cheerily.

'The rain,' she replied. It was battering away at the window. 'Rain's the best kind of weather, it's so subversive, it messes up everything.' She suddenly turned round and noticed what was round my neck.

'I thought you'd burnt that hideous scarf weeks ago.'

'No, no, it's still about . . . and I decided I'd better wear it today as I shall be seeing Nan . . . anyway I just looked in to say I'm off in a minute.'

'Well, go on then,' she said, in a very weary voice. 'Run back to Daddy. I bet you can't wait to suck up to him again.'

'Now that's rather unfair,' I protested.

She got up and faced me. 'No it isn't. I've seen you weakening. You're going right back to your creepy old ways.' Her voice rose accusingly. 'You didn't want to join in the strike against Tinkler, did you?'

I hesitated.

'Go on, admit it.'

'Well, no, I didn't, because he's really not all that bad.'

'What!' she shrieked.

'He's made some massive mistakes, especially with you. But I think he knows that now and if we just give him a chance—'

'Oh, just leave before I start throwing up,' she cried. 'Go on, clear off. I've finished with you.'

Her words walloped me. I stood there smarting before bursting out, 'You talk

189

about adults wanting to control us all the time, but you're just the same. I mustn't carry an umbrella. I can't wear the scarf that I like. I can never talk to a teacher voluntarily . . . so many rules. You know what, I'm just as much of a bod now as I was before. Only now I'm doing everything *you* tell me. And, by the way, I don't think people are either bods or troublemakers. There can't just be two types of people—'

'You know what, I really couldn't care less,' yelled Miranda, waving a dismissive hand.

'Oh, I know that,' I yelled back. 'I've just got to bow down and obey you all the time.'

Miranda had turned her back on me now but I still ranted on. 'A true friend is someone who will like me for who I am, even if I'm not quite sure who that is yet. But you just see me as some kind of experiment, not a real person at all—'

Suddenly Miranda whirled round, hurt flashing across her face. She shot past me, charged down the stairs and banged the front door in an extremely forceful way.

Julia came upstairs. 'She's been in such a funny mood these last couple of days . . . I think she's upset you're going. Don't worry, she'll come round.'

I doubted it. I'd said some very sharp things to her. And I regretted every one of them now.

Dad arrived, and we packed up the car. When we got home, he gave me a massive hug. I felt as if I'd just returned from a far-off planet.

10.00 p.m.
Dad, Nan and I went out for a celebratory meal this evening. We'd just sat down at our table when this woman came over and asked Dad if he was in *Rivals*. When he said, yes, her face lit up, and she handed him a scrap of paper to sign.

'My first ever autograph,' said Dad, in a wondering kind of way afterwards.

SUNDAY APRIL 5TH
Nan left this morning. But Dad promised we'd go and visit her on my birthday, which is very soon now.

'Don't forget to get my room ready,' I said.

'It's all ready now love,' she replied.

This afternoon I rang Miranda all set to offer my heartfelt apologies. But she put the phone down on me.

What have I done?

MONDAY APRIL 6TH

At school I went up to Miranda – who was scowling fiercely at anyone who dared come near her – and said, 'I would like to thank you for all your help. It has been invaluable.' I wanted to add that I couldn't have got through these last weeks without her wisdom and energy – but I never got the chance.

She snapped, 'From now on I'm only helping animals. Humans are nothing but trouble,' and strode away.

Couldn't she see I was brimming with remorse?

TUESDAY APRIL 7TH

Last day of term.

Mr Tinkler loosened up a little bit in lessons today. He's gone on being polite to Miranda too. Everyone's noticed. I told him I was back living with my dad now, and he looked really pleased.

At the end of the day I wished Miranda a happy holiday. She blanked me. How much longer will she be this hostile? Has she forgotten all our good times?

WEDNESDAY APRIL 8TH

Dad saw Cheryl tonight. He was only gone a couple of hours. Afterwards he was rather shame-faced about it all. But I am perfectly content for him to have meetings with Cheryl, I just do not want her living here again. So I said. 'It's quite enjoyable having friends of the opposite sex, isn't it? How about inviting Cheryl round for a meal on Saturday?' Dad seems amazed by my new sophistication. I'm pretty amazed too.

THURSDAY APRIL 9TH

Dad's offered to take me to the set of *Rivals* one day, so I can watch the filming. That would be really excellent. He also said I could bring a friend. At once I thought of Miranda and then felt deeply depressed again.

FRIDAY APRIL 10TH

A few reflections about Miranda.

She burst into my life like a shooting star, shattering my staid existence. Now she's as far away from me as the furthest planet in the universe.

I miss her every minute that ticks by. Too depressed to write any more.

SATURDAY APRIL 11TH

10.30 p.m.

Cheryl came round for dinner tonight. I asked her if she had any culinary wishes. She replied she was happy to leave the food entirely to me. I'm pleased to say she cleared her plate and pronounced it 'extremely delicious', which indeed it was.

Felt dead tired afterwards. It wasn't just the cooking. It was the mental strain as well. After she'd gone Dad watched me clearing up in the kitchen. I could tell he was wrestling with some powerful emotions. Finally, he said huskily, 'You were top class tonight, Archie.'

11.15 p.m.

How about if I give Miranda an Easter egg tomorrow? I know she's a bit of a chocolate fiend.

Could this be the way to restore our friendship?

SUNDAY APRIL 12TH

Delivered Miranda's Easter egg today. It was one of the biggest in the shop. I wasn't showing off, I just wanted Miranda to see how badly I wished to resume friendly relations.

Julia opened the door and instantly invited me inside. We had a great reunion. Then I explained about my offering for Miranda. She rushed off to get her. She was gone ages, which I thought was ominous. She returned alone. 'I'm very sorry, but Miranda can't come down at the moment.'

I pretended to believe this and said, 'Would you mind giving Miranda this chocolate egg, with the compliments of the season, please?'

'Of course,' said Julia. 'It's most kind of you.'

'Would you also tell Miranda that it's my birthday on Friday. I shall be leaving to visit my nan at eleven o'clock – but if Miranda would care to come round and toast my birthday . . .'

'I'll tell her, Archie.'

Then, just as I was leaving Julia invited me back to have a cup of tea with her. She said, 'Be patient Archie, she's not as tough as she lets on. Miranda's trouble is that she's always been compared to her sister. Teachers would say to me, "She's not Claire, is she?" And I'd think, well, of course she's not and I wouldn't want her to be either. Just let her be herself.'

She added, in a conspiratorial whisper, 'She and I have had our ups and downs but lately we'd been getting on so much better. Only now ... well, she's totally withdrawn from everything these last few days.'

She looked so upset I explained that Miranda knew about the child tamer.

'I just wanted some help before Miranda disappeared down the dark tunnel of adolescence,' she explained. Then she thanked me for letting her know.

I have done the right thing telling her, haven't I? My life is so complicated at the moment.

MONDAY APRIL 13TH
Thought Miranda might have rung to thank me for the Easter egg. But she didn't. She is obviously still brooding on what I'd said in the heat of the moment.

I have a feeling Miranda may brood about things for a very long time. So we'll probably start talking again sometime in the sixth form.

WEDNESDAY APRIL 15TH
Discussed my plight regarding Miranda with Dad tonight. He put down his script

and listened to me with keen interest. He said, rather sadly, he didn't think there was anything else I could do. It was up to her now.

I was grateful for his insights but not exactly cheered up by them. Still, I'm keeping busy. I made up a new rota today. Dad says he wants to do his fair share this time. I'm also reading up on some new recipes. I'm determined to move forward, even if it is with an exceptionally heavy heart.

FRIDAY APRIL 17TH
11.15 a.m.

Something incredible has just happened and I must record it right away.

This morning I waited for Miranda to come and toast my birthday. But I waited in vain. Not even my presents could soften my aching disappointment. Then, just as eleven o'clock was striking, the doorbell rang.

I leaped to the door and there was Miranda – dressed up as me, just as she had been that day at school. Once again there was an umbrella under one arm, a newspaper under the other. Her school uniform was immaculate, with every button done up. She'd even exhumed the huge and faintly smelly scarf she'd worn before.

'Good morning,' she said, in a rather good impression of my voice.

'Playing along I said, 'Hello Archie, how are you?'

'My health is perfectly satisfactory, thank you,' said Miranda. 'Miranda refuses to come and see you on your birthday. She's sulking, but she has asked me to deliver a present to you.'

'Very generous of her,' I said.

'It's dead stingy of her actually, because it's second-hand.' She thrust into my hand one of the friendship bracelets she'd worn on her arm almost every day since I'd known her.

I gaped at it in amazement. 'But I can't take this.'

'Well, I'm not taking it back . . . you know what a temper that Miranda's got.'

'But this was given to her by her boyfriend,' I protested.

'I can tell you a secret about that, if you'd care to hear it.'

'Yes please.'

'Don't breathe a word to anyone, but actually, she bought that bracelet for herself. She only pretended a boyfriend gave it to her.'

I couldn't stop this smile from spreading right across my face.

'So you do still want it?' she demanded.

'Of course I do . . . I'll wear it until it rots on my arm.'

'You're mad,' she said, in her own voice and suddenly turned away. She made as if to leave.

'Just one thing,' I said.

I went over to her and took away the umbrella. 'Archie doesn't usually carry one of these now. Also . . .' I undid her top button, 'he often has this undone now. He's even been known to undo two buttons some days. He's changed a lot.'

'So I see,' said Miranda. 'I wouldn't want him to change too much, though. I sort of like the way he wears hideous scarves and does totally uncool things like tap-dancing – that shows he's an individual. Only I would like it if he'd give me a few days warning when he's planning his next dance attack in assembly. I need to be prepared for something so utterly gruesome. So when is he, I mean, when are you – back from your nan's?'

'Thursday afternoon.'

'What are you doing on Thursday night?'
'Nothing.'
'You are now. You're having tea round at my house. See you about six o'clock. Bye.'

A Reply From Aunty Prue

Dear Miranda,

Thanks for your latest letter and sorry for the delay in replying. I had a large number of letters waiting for me when I got back from my holiday.

I'm so glad you and Archie are getting on better now. There's more to everyone – including ourselves – than we realize. I'm so glad you've found that out.

Best wishes for the future.

Aunty Prue

MIRANDA JONES

Aunty Prue
Problem Solver Page
WOW
Williams Terrace
London

Friday April 24th

Dear Aunty Prue,
   Cheers for replying at long last. Two
things to tell you.
   Firstly Archie. He came round my
house yesterday for tea. He also bought
me a present: a friendship bracelet. I'm
wearing it on my wrist now, if you
want to know.
   Secondly, I have been spending some
time with the saggy and the mad (i.e.
my mum). She'd been paying a woman to
tell her how to talk to me! Had a long

row with her about that. But then I had a brainwave. I said, 'Mum, why don't you just chop her out, thereby saving yourself lots of money – which you can donate to me if you like – and we can go on talking like this.'

So that's what we've started doing.

And another thing, I appeared on telly tonight (don't you love the casual way I just slipped that in?). Last week I was waiting in this TV station foyer with Archie to meet his dad, when this excitable man came flapping over to us. He was about to start filming a discussion programme for teenagers but had been let down at the 'eleventh hour'. Did either of us feel strongly about anything?

Archie just froze but I shot on to that programme and never shut up. Watching myself tonight was dead embarrassing – all I could see was this gigantic nose. But Mum went into raptures. 'I could never have spoken so fluently,' she said, 'and neither could Claire.'

I've actually out-classed Claire at something. Can you believe that? And they want me back on that show. So, if you like watching big noses, tune in. I'll let you know the date.

Now, I'm going to help you, Aunty Prue. From your letter you sound a bit tired and over-worked. What you need is a partner. Well, look no further. I've realized that I really enjoy helping people and I'm very good at it, too. So I can answer some of your letters for you. I bet that's cheered you up, hasn't it?

I don't want to be called 'Aunty' though - too corny. No, I'll just be Miranda. And I shall be extremely frank in my replies.

What do you think?

Thanking you in anticipation of a quick reply - tomorrow would be great.

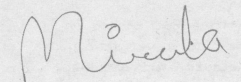

Miranda (alias Troublemaker!)

RESCUING DAD
Pete Johnson

'How do you improve your dad?'

Joe and Claire can see why Mum chucked Dad out. He looks a mess, he can't cook and he's useless around the house. Something must be done: they're the only ones who can help transform him into 'Dad Mark Two'. And when they unveil this new, improved dad, Mum will be so impressed she'll take him back on the spot!

But then disaster strikes – Mum starts seeing the slimy and creepy Roger. And Joe and Claire's plans take an unexpected turn – with hilarious results.

'Pete Johnson is a wonderful story-teller'
Evening Standard

ISBN 0 440 86457 7

HOW TO TRAIN
YOUR PARENTS
Pete Johnson

They think I'M a big problem. Wrong.
THEY are!

Louis can't handle it any more. His new school is Swotsville and his mum and dad have fallen into some very bad ways. All they seem to care about now is how well he's doing at school (answer: not well) and what after-school clubs he wants to join (answer: none!). They're no longer interested in his jokes (his dream is to be a comedian) and have even nicked the telly out of his bedroom!

What's going on? And can new friend Maddy help? For Maddy tells him her parents used to behave equally badly until she trained them. All parents have to be trained – and she knows a foolproof way...

'Pete Johnson has created a boy who makes you laugh out loud.' *Sunday Times*

ISBN 0 440 86439 9

AVENGER
Pete Johnson

I can't ever forget what you did! This is war!

Gareth is delighted when Jake, the new boy who's full of exciting tales befriends him – but when Gareth is caught doing an impression of Jake's accent, everything changes. Jakes is furious and determined to have his revenge! Gareth has to draw on the memory of his beloved Grandad, and on the only thing he has left of him – the magical mysterious Avenger mask that Grandad wore when he was a wrestler. But is Jake really the opponent he seems to be?

A spellbinding thriller about revenge, forgiveness and a very special friendship.

'It's a brilliant read' *Sunday Express*

ISBN 0 440 86458 5